**Sister Adelaide Peters stood in front of Professor Coenraad van Essen, trying to be composed and cool, and to forget his kiss amidst the ruins of the bus; his fee, he had called it.**

"I must thank you for getting me out last night. I was very frightened, you know. It was so dark. I believe you saved our lives, and I am indeed grateful. Just thanking you doesn't seem enough," she added worriedly.

"Thanking me is quite enough, Sister Peters. It just so happened that I was there. It could have been anyone else, you know." She felt surprised at this.

"But I knew it would be you." The professor was studying the papers before him, his pen busy once more, and she didn't expect an answer. She gave a small, unconscious sigh.

"Did you and Dr. Beekman sleep last night? You both look very tired."

"It was hardly worth it, Sister. We'll go off early if we can." He glanced up from his work, half smiling. "Thank you for you solicitude. Now, if you are ready, shall we have the next patient?"

Romance readers around the world were sad to note the passing of **Betty Neels** in June 2001. Her career spanned thirty years, and she continued to write into her ninetieth year. To her millions of fans, Betty epitomized the romance writer, and yet she began writing almost by accident. She had retired from nursing, but her inquiring mind still sought stimulation. Her new career was born when she heard a lady in her local library bemoaning the lack of good romance novels. Betty's first book, *Sister Peters in Amsterdam,* was published in 1969, and she eventually completed 134 books. Her novels offer a reassuring warmth that was very much a part of her own personality. She was a wonderful writer, and she will be greatly missed. Her spirit and genuine talent will live on in all her stories.

THE BEST *of*

# BETTY NEELS

## SISTER PETERS IN AMSTERDAM

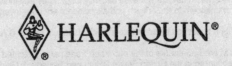

# HARLEQUIN®

TORONTO • NEW YORK • LONDON
AMSTERDAM • PARIS • SYDNEY • HAMBURG
STOCKHOLM • ATHENS • TOKYO • MILAN • MADRID
PRAGUE • WARSAW • BUDAPEST • AUCKLAND

ISBN-13: 978-0-373-47079-2
ISBN-10:     0-373-47079-7

SISTER PETERS IN AMSTERDAM

# CHAPTER ONE

IT was one o'clock, the corridor leading from the main hospital to the Children's Unit was very quiet. As Matron accompanied the professor to the ward, her thoughts were busy. She knew that the morning clinics were over; Sister Peters would be back from lunch and the children should be quiet enough for him to have a talk with her, before making his decision.

When the exchange plan had first been suggested by the Grotehof Hospital in Amsterdam, her own hospital committee had had no hesitation in recommending Sister Peters, who was in charge of Children's Casualty and Out-Patients as well as the ward. However, she had hardly expected matters to have gone forward as rapidly as they had. The professor had arrived within a few hours of his conversation with her, and she had had no time to speak to Sister Peters. She hoped that everything would go smoothly. As they reached the glass doors of the ward, she looked at the tall man beside her; he seemed very pleasant; rather quiet perhaps, but he had a charming voice and spoke excellent English. He did not open the doors but stood watching the girl sitting on a low chair with her back to them. She wore a shapeless white gown over her uniform, but the frilled cap—a dainty affair of spotted muslin—perched on top of a coil of vivid red hair, showed her rank. She had just put down a feeding bottle on the table before her, as she hoisted a fat baby on to her shoulder. She patted his back while he glared at them through the door. Presently he gave a loud burp and was rewarded by a light kiss on the top of his head as he was neatly tucked under her arm while she stooped to lift a fallen toddler to its feet again. As she stood up, two small children ran over to her and caught hold of her apron and toddled beside her as she went over to the cots. The doors squeaked as the professor opened them, but she didn't look around.

'I'm all behind, Nurse.' She spoke in a clear, unworried voice. 'Johnny's been sick again. I popped him into a bath and put him back to bed. He'd better be seen as soon as I can get someone.' She tucked the baby expertly into his cot, picked up one of the toddlers and looked over her shoulder. She was surprised to see Matron, but remained unruffled. Still holding the child, she went across the ward to her. She was a pretty girl, with large brown eyes, extravagantly fringed with black lashes, a small straight nose and a wide mouth, nicely turned up at the corners. She was smiling as she spoke to Matron.

'Good afternoon, Matron. I'm sorry, I didn't hear you come in.' Matron returned her smile.

'Good afternoon, Sister. Have you no nurses on duty?'

'The clinics were late this morning, Matron. Nurses are all at second dinner; they'll be back any minute now.'

She glanced at the man standing so quietly at Matron's side. She supposed he was a visiting doctor looking around the hospital, and wondered why he chose to come at such an awkward time. Matron's next words cut across her thoughts.

'Sister, this is Professor van Essen, senior consultant pediatrician at the Grotehof Hospital in Amsterdam.' She paused. 'He is just taking a look round.' She tuned to him. 'Professor, this is Sister Peters.'

The girl put out her hand. 'How do you do, sir?' She smiled at him in a friendly way, and thought how handsome he was in a dark, beaky-nosed fashion.

The professor shook hands and returned her smile, saying only, 'How do you do' in a rather formal way. He caught Matron's eye.

'May I go round with Sister, Matron? That is, if she can spare the time.'

He waited patiently while Sister Peters took off her gown, handed the toddlers over to a nurse who had just come in, and put on her cuffs. Having ad-

justed these to a nicety, she indicated her readiness
to conduct him around the ward. His tour was a
thorough one, his questions searching and numerous. Sister Peters began to think that he would
never go, and blushed guiltily when he said at
length:

'Forgive me for taking up so much of your time,
Sister. I do have an excellent reason for doing so,
and that must be my excuse.' He hesitated, and she
thought he was going to say more; instead he
smiled at her so charmingly that she felt a distinct
stab of regret when he left the ward.

She wondered about him once or twice during
the rest of the day and so far forgot herself as to
day-dream about him—something quite alien to her
nature, for she was a sensible young woman who
accepted her life cheerfully and made the most of
it. Only persistent cries of 'Adelaide, it's your turn
to make the tea' from the other occupants of the
Sisters' sitting room brought her back to reality,
and as she jumped to her feet to put the kettle on,
she told herself not to waste her time on such
senseless mooning. This sensible attitude of mind,
however, did not last very long, and her last
thoughts before she slept that night were of the professor from Holland.

Coenraad van Essen, walking back with Matron
to her office, assured her that he considered Sister

Peters would be most suitable for the post in his hospital. Matron nodded her agreement.

'Sister is a first-class nurse,' she said. 'She's young, I know, barely twenty-five, but she has had several years' experience and is especially good with children in Out-Patients and Casualty, and I understand that she will be working for you in those departments at your clinic.'

'Will she object to living in Holland for a year? Has she family ties or—er—is she engaged to be married?'

Matron reassured him. 'Sister is the daughter of a country parson, she has twin brothers younger than herself—still at school, I believe. They are a devoted family, but I see no reason why she should not go to Holland, for to the best of my knowledge she is not engaged. She's a very popular girl, but shy, and makes no effort to attract attention.'

'There could hardly be any need to do so,' murmured the professor, 'with that hair.'

Matron looked rather taken aback. 'It is rather striking,' she conceded, 'but I can assure you that whatever the colour of her hair, Sister Peters is ideally suited for the post.'

They parted on the friendliest of terms, arranging to meet in Matron's office in the morning, as the professor had expressed a wish to be present when Sister Peters was offered the job. It was almost nine o'clock the next morning when the phone rang, and

Adelaide, who had been half expecting a summons, answered it. It was Matron. 'Sister Peters, would you come to my office at once, please?' She answered with a meek 'Yes, Matron,' and thought uneasily of the noisy toddlers and untidy ward yesterday afternoon, which Matron would not have failed to observe. Perhaps the professor had remarked on it, although he had appeared oblivious of the chaos and noise around him. 'And so he should,' thought Adelaide. 'If he runs a children's clinic he must know that they shout and yell and vomit and wet their nappies, irrespective of Matron or doctors' rounds.' She smoothed her apron, put on her cuffs and patted the cap on her astonishing hair, told the staff nurse where she was going, and set off for the office.

When she knocked and went in, the professor rose from the arm of the chair where he had been sitting, and she returned his greeting with a rather startled good morning as she went across the room to Matron's desk. She eyed that lady warily. She appeared to be in a good humour, but with Matron that didn't always signify; she could deliver a telling set-down in the friendliest possible way. Adelaide stole a look at the professor, lounging against the mantelpiece, with his hands in his pockets. He was looking at her and smiling almost as though he read her thoughts. She bit her lip and went a little pink as she dutifully gave Matron her full attention.

'You have doubtless heard of the exchange scheme between this hospital and the Grotehof Hospital in Amsterdam, Sister.' Matron looked at Adelaide, but gave her no time to reply. 'As you know, an arrangement has been made for our two hospitals to exchange a member of our staff for a period of one year. The hospital committee has decided to nominate you, and I must say that much as we shall miss you, I must endorse their choice. Professor Van Essen feels that you will be most satisfactory for the post of Out-Patients and Casualty sister in his clinic—it only remains for you to decide if you will accept the offer.'

Matron rounded off this speech with an encouraging smile and nod. Adelaide, who had been listening with growing surprise and excitement, was still trying to find her voice when the professor spoke.

'Before you say anything, Sister Peters, I should like you to know that I and my staff will be very happy to welcome you at the clinic, and will do our best to make you happy as well as keep you busy while you are with us,' he smiled down at her. 'Please say that you will come.'

Adelaide looked up at him. She liked his quiet, unhurried voice, she liked his face. He was very good-looking, she decided, but good looks didn't count with her. His nose was certainly very beaky; she wondered why he wore glasses. His eyes were twinkling now, and she saw his lips twitch, and realised that she had been staring. She bit her lip. 'I'm sorry,' she stammered. 'Quite understandable, Sister,' he smiled. Adelaide made up her mind. She liked the professor, and rather to her own surprise, for she was not a hasty girl, found herself accepting his offer without further preamble.

'Good, Sister Peters. I will leave Matron to make all the necessary arrangements, and shall hope to see you in due course.'

'Well, that's settled.' Matron sounded pleased. 'You will want to go back to your ward now, Sister. Perhaps you will come and see me this afternoon, and I will tell you all the details then.'

Adelaide thanked her, and repeated her thanks rather shyly to the professor as he held the door open for her. He said nothing further, however, only smiled briefly.

Her mind was in a whirl as she walked back to the Children's Unit. Perhaps she should have taken more time to decide, but the professor had seemed so sure of her acceptance that it had seemed quite natural to say yes immediately. She felt a thrill of excitement. She hoped that Dutch wasn't too difficult a language, for she supposed that she would have to learn it if she was to make a success of her new job. It suddenly seemed most important that she should do well and please the professor.

# CHAPTER TWO

As Adelaide walked towards the Children's Clinic at eight o'clock on the morning of her first day in Amsterdam, the professor was coming down the staircase of his lovely old house on the Heerengracht. Below him he could see Castor and Pollux, his two labrador dogs, sitting side by side, waiting for him to take them for their morning walk. As he crossed the black and white tiled hall he gave a cheerful good morning to his butler, Tweedle, who looked up from the coat he was brushing.

'Good morning, Mr Coenraad.' He looked at his master over his old-fashioned spectacles. 'You'll need to wear a coat.' He spoke in English, with the respectful familiarity of the old family servant and friend. The professor, born the Baron Coenraad Blankenaar van Essen, and possessed of a considerable fortune, would always be 'Mr Coenraad' to Tweedle and his wife, who acted as the professor's housekeeper. The butler's earliest recollections of Coenraad had been the conversations they had held with each other as he opened the great front door to allow the small boy and his even smaller sisters to go through on their way to the park or to school. The professor stood waiting patiently for his coat. He was polishing his glasses and looked quite different without them, and considerably younger. His eyes, bright and searching, were blue-grey.

'Any news?' he asked, as he put on his coat. Tweedle eased it over the broad shoulders.

'Freule Keizer telephoned and asked me to remind you that she expects you to take her to the Concertgebouw this evening.'

The professor frowned. 'I suppose I must have said I would take her. Oh, well, I can't disappoint an old friend.'

He had known Margriet Keizer since childhood. She was now a handsome young woman, and there had been some speculation among their friends as to whether they intended to marry. She was suitable in every way and would make an admirable wife for the professor, as she had been at some pains to let him realise, but so far he had remained a good friend and nothing more. All the same, Tweedle, who disliked her, was very much afraid that he would marry her sooner or later, even if only for the sake of an heir.

Coenraad, threading the Volvo through the early morning traffic, was not thinking of Margriet, however. Today, the English Sister would be at the clinic for the first time. He hoped that he had made a wise choice—she had seemed exactly the type of girl they had been hoping for, but there was always the language difficulty. Even with lessons it would be a few weeks before she could make herself understood. It would be interesting to see how she would make out.

He parked the car and strode rapidly through the Vondelpark, the two dogs careering ahead, making the most of their half hour's run. Back home, the professor read his post and glanced at the papers as he ate his breakfast. At precisely ten minutes to nine he left his home for the hospital. There he left his coat and gloves in the changing room, and walked down the familiar corridor. His registrar, Piet Beekman, came out of Casualty as he passed. They were friends of long standing. Piet was the professor's junior by five years and married to a nurse. They had a baby son, and Coenraad was the little boy's godfather, and a frequent visitor to their flat. They said '*Dag*' briefly and Piet fell into step beside his chief.

'She's here, the English girl—I've not seen her, but Staff Nurse Wilsma says she's nice, but has the most frightful red hair.'

The professor nodded, only half listening, his thoughts already busy with the day's work. They went through the door Piet had opened, into his office. Adelaide and the staff nurse had their backs to him as he entered. She looked very small and slight beside the sturdy Dutch girl. The two girls turned round as Piet closed the door, and came towards the doctors. Adelaide gave an inward sigh of relief; the professor was exactly as she had remembered him—no, that wasn't true; he was even better. They smiled at each other and shook hands, and Piet Beekman was introduced.

'You'll find the routine here very similar to your hospital in London, Sister Peters. Dr Beekman and I will speak English with you until your Dutch is adequate. I understand lessons are already arranged?'

As he himself had sought out an old friend of his father and persuaded him to give Adelaide lessons, the question was an unnecessary one, but Adelaide, who was feeling shy in her strange surroundings, was glad to be able to talk about the arrangements which had been made for her.

She had enjoyed the hour before the professor had arrived. Staff Nurse had taken her over the clinic and she had opened and shut drawers and peered into cupboards and examined trolleys, and drawn the conclusion that Casualty at least was almost identical with its English counterpart. She thought that, even with the language barrier, she would be able to manage quite well. She liked the nurses. Zuster Wilsma was a little younger than herself, a big jolly girl, blonde and blue-eyed. She had been at the clinic for a year now, and although her English was fragmental, Adelaide guessed that

she was going to be a great help to her. Nurse
Eisink was the senior student nurse, as dark as
Zuster Wilsma was fair, and only half her size. She
had enormous pale blue eyes and a very attractive
smile. The third nurse, Zuster Steensma, was the
junior, a thick-set, stolid girl with black boot-button
eyes and blonde hair that she obviously didn't
bother about a great deal. She beamed at Adelaide,
who beamed back. She was quite undeterred by
their inability to communicate excepting on the
most basic terms. It seemed to her that she was very
lucky; they all seemed so anxious to be friendly
and helpful.

The desk in the professor's office was, however,
a different matter. The forms upon it were not in
the least like those to which she had been used, and
the printing on them was quite incomprehensible to
her. She determined to stay on that evening and
study them. They were of various colours; if she
was very careful to watch during the clinics, she
should be able to identify them later, and learn their
various uses. The Dutch she had heard so far had
been quite beyond her; indeed, by nine o'clock, a
dozen small worries and doubts had assailed her,
but somehow the sight of the professor's placid
face and his firm handshake had done much to put
her fears at rest. She liked Dr Beekman too, he
looked good-natured and cheerful. He was nearly
as tall as the professor, but of a burlier build, with

very fair hair and blue eyes. He spoke English with fluency, but with a terrible accent.

The professor asked her gravely if she could say '*Ja*' and '*Neen*', and everyone laughed, and she felt quite at ease. He noted this as he was putting on his white coat; it seemed the right moment to start work; he signed to Zuster Wilsma to bring in the first little patient, and work started.

The clinics finished for the day at five o'clock, and the doctors left together. The professor was very well satisfied with the day's work; Adelaide, despite her difficulties with the language, had managed well. She had not been easily flustered or put out. As he took off his coat he congratulated her on getting through the day so competently, and told her to go and enjoy her evening, for she had earned it. Adelaide wished them both a cheerful goodbye, and they went on their way; Piet Beekman to his home, the professor to do a round of his private patients in the town.

Adelaide stood where they had left her, thinking about the professor. She liked him, very much. The thought that she would be working with him every day for a whole year was an extremely pleasant one. She finished clearing up and went along to Casualty. Staff Nurse had just come on duty, and would be there until the night staff arrived. Adelaide said goodnight and went back along the corridor to the office, went inside, and shut the

door. She was off duty, no one need know that she
was there. She was determined to study the forms
and papers lying on the desk; she had had to be
told a dozen times during the day which was
needed. She wondered how the doctors had managed to keep their patience with her. It wasn't going to happen again. She sat down on the professor's chair, got out her dictionary and notebook,
and set to work. It was far worse than she had
anticipated—it meant looking up every word, one
at a time, and she hadn't known that the Dutch
liked their verbs at the end of their sentences, and
not in the middle. By the end of an hour she had
sorted out the forms and had learnt what they were
for, but she had no idea how to pronounce the
words she had so carefully learned to write. Someone had told her—in England before she left—that
if she pronounced every letter in a Dutch word, she
would be understood, but had omitted to tell her
that the Dutch alphabet didn't sound the same as
the English one anyway; so she sat, happily and
painstakingly mispronouncing every word.

She was heard by the professor, on his way back
from seeing an urgent case in the children's ward.
As he passed his office he saw the light beneath
the door and wondered idly who was there. He decided to have a look, and it was his rather startled
gaze which met Adelaide's eye as she looked up

from his desk. She was trying to say *Geneeskundige Dienst*, and getting in an appalling muddle.

The professor shut the door. 'That's rather a difficult word for you to cut your teeth on, you know.'

Adelaide jumped up. She looked surprised, but not in the least disconcerted. In reply to the professor's enquiry as to whether she wasn't off duty, she said:

'Yes, I am, sir, but I want to learn these forms before tomorrow. I was a great hindrance to you today.'

She watched the professor take off his topcoat and draw up a chair, waving her back into his at the same time.

'I don't think you have the pronunciation quite right,' he remarked mildly. 'Do you know what all these are?' He waved at the mass of papers on the desk.

'Oh, yes, sir. I've got them all written down, and when I have a lesson with Mijnheer de Wit, tomorrow, I shall ask him to teach me how to say them correctly.'

The professor took out his pipe. 'Do you mind if I smoke?'

She looked surprised and shook her head.

'It occurs to me that it would be to the advantage of all of us if you learn the pronunciation now, Sister Peters.'

Adelaide gathered her books together and started

to get up. In this she was thwarted by the professor's hand, and was forced to sit down again, protesting, 'I really cannot let you waste your time like this, sir.' She sounded rather prim. She had never met a member of the consultant staff who behaved quite as he was, and she wasn't quite sure what to do. He did not appear to have heard her, but reached for the phone and told the operator to get his home. When Tweedle answered, he looked at the clock. He had almost forgotten Margriet.

'Tweedle? Will you ring Freule Keizer and tell her that I'm unavoidably detained. I'll pick her up at the end of the concert and take her home.'

He grinned at Tweedle's sigh of satisfaction; he was well aware of the old man's feelings about Margriet. Adelaide, watching him, wondered why he smiled, and started to protest at his spoilt evening.

'I didn't want to go anyway,' he said. 'It was a Bach concert, I should have gone to sleep.'

Adelaide laughed, and he asked briskly:

'When do you have supper? Eight o'clock? Good, we have three-quarters of an hour. We will take one form at a time.'

He worked her hard, with a merciless criticism which made her blush and stammer, but at the end of the allotted time she had mastered the medical terms well enough to be understood. As she collected her books together, she thanked him, and added:

'I hope you will have a very pleasant evening, sir,' to which he made no reply, merely holding the door politely for her to pass through. When she reached her room she got out her dictionary once more and looked up '*Freule*'. It said 'an unmarried female member of the nobility.' She would be tall and blonde, Adelaide decided, and very beautiful. Her clothes would be exquisite. Adelaide hated her. Doubtless the professor admired blondes. She tugged at her own red mane as she tidied herself for supper, and jabbed the pins in with a complete disregard for the pain she was giving herself.

She longed to ask some questions at supper, but conversation, although friendly, was of necessity limited. She sat, listened to the unintelligible chatter around her, and wondered what the professor was doing. He was still in his office, having been delayed by a phone call from Tweedle reminding him that he still hadn't had his dinner. He lighted his pipe and reached for his coat, and went in search of his car. It had been a long day; he yawned, and hoped that Margriet wasn't going to be too maddeningly boring about Bach.

Adelaide loved Amsterdam. On her second evening at the hospital, Zuster Zijlstra had walked with her to the Spui, where Mijnheer de Wit lived. They

went through the Kalverstraat, and had found time
to take a quick look at the shops, gay with pretty
clothes and jewellery and silverware. Zuster Zijlstra
rang the bell of the small gabled house and, when
the door opened, waved Adelaide a cheerful goodbye. Adelaide, left to herself, pushed the door wider
and heard a voice telling her to come upstairs. She
climbed several steep flights before she saw who
had spoken to her. An elderly white-haired man
was standing on the tiny landing. He introduced
himself and led her into his flat. Here, he wasted
no time, but took her hat and coat, sat her down at
the table, and plunged into her first lesson. Rather
to her dismay, he spoke Dutch, only using English
when he saw that she was completely befogged. At
the end of an hour he wished her a polite good
night, and sent her back with a great deal of homework. He seemed pleased with her, but Adelaide
thought that she would have to work very hard indeed to keep him so.

Zuster Zijlstra and Zuster Boot, from Men's Sur-
gical, both spoke a little English. They took Adelaide shopping as often as possible during the next
few days; the feast of St Nicolaas was only a few
weeks away. They explained that she should give
small gifts to the doctors and nurses she was working with, and also explained the enormous numbers
of chocolate letters displayed in the confectioners'
and *banketbakker*. It seemed that it was customary

to exchange them with friends and relations. Zuster Boot, a practical young woman, volunteered to supply the christian names of the clinic nurses so that Adelaide could buy the appropriate letters for them; she already knew that she must get a C for the professor, and a P for Piet Beekman. They roamed from shop to shop in their off-duty, choosing scarves and stockings and fancy soap, and admiring the lovely things on display. When they were off duty in the afternoons they went to Formosa in the Kalverstraat, where Adelaide sampled *thé complet*; she was enchanted with the tray of savoury tit-bits and cream cakes and chocolates, with its accompanying pot of tea.

Just before St Nicolaas, she and Staff Nurse Wilsma spent an hour choosing presents for the two doctors. Dr Beekman was easy; he never had a pen of his own. They chose a vivid green one he couldn't possibly mislay. The professor was rather more difficult; he seemed to have everything. In the end they settled for a leather wallet. Wilsma was sure that he had several already, but observed that he could always put it away and use it later.

There was no clinic on the morning of St Nicolaas. Instead the nurses and porters set about transforming the Out-Patients' waiting hall. Paper chains and flags hung around the walls, and tables were set up, covered with gay cloths and loaded with glasses and plates and great baskets of oranges. The annual party for the hospital's small patients was to be held that afternoon. St Nicolaas and Black Pete would be coming to distribute the presents. Adelaide, opening tins of biscuits, asked, 'Who gives this party, Zuster Wilsma?'

Her staff nurse, scooping sweets into countless little bags, stopped her work to reply. 'Professor Van Essen. He pays for it all too. He'll be coming, and his aunt and sisters—he's got two, and his nephews and nieces—and his close friends'—she looked at Adelaide, and added, 'and Dr Beekman and his wife and baby.'

Adelaide hadn't understood half of what Zuster Wilsma had said, but there wasn't time for explanations, anyway. They still had to fill several sacks with presents.

At two o'clock the first guests arrived; most of them had mothers or big sisters with them. Adelaide sat the children in rows on the floor; the grown-ups lined the walls. Presently Zuster Zijlstra arrived, opened the piano, and started to play the first of the traditional tunes, and everyone began to sing. Adelaide didn't understand a word, but when St Nicolaas appeared with his black slave, she laughed and clapped with everyone else, and carried the smallest toddlers up to receive their presents. She was enjoying herself enormously. At length the Saint made his stately exit, sent on his way by enthusiastic and rather shrill singing.

Adelaide dumped the baby she was holding into the nearest nurse's lap and went over to the tables to pour lemonade and hand out biscuits.

There was no lack of helpers; she piled the oranges in baskets ready for the nurses to take round, talking all the while to Zuster Zijlstra in her mixture of Dutch and English. It was at this moment that the professor, with his aunt and sisters, chose to join them. They all seemed to know Zuster Zijlstra, and greeted her like an old friend. Adelaide, started to move quietly away, but the professor, who had been expecting her to do just that, put out a detaining hand and turned her smartly round, and performed his introductions in English.

She found herself the centre of an animated group. His two sisters were very like him, with dark hair and blue eyes; they wore their elegant clothes with a careless grace. His aunt was small and slim and just as elegant as her nieces. She eyed Adelaide with bright black eyes and talked to her in a gentle voice. They were all charming to her and chattered and laughed until they were presently joined by several children, who addressed the professor as Uncle, and smiled shyly at Adelaide as he introduced them. When, after a little while, they all bade her goodbye. Adelaide watched them go with regret; it seemed unlikely that she would meet them again.

The professor made no attempt to go with them. Adelaide hesitated.

'I must go and help the others; I'm not doing my share. It was delightful meeting your family, Professor.'

She was about to turn away when an attractive young woman put her hand on the professor's arm. Adelaide looked at her. This must be Margriet. At once, and irrationally, she disliked her. Freule Keizer was extremely good-looking, with blonde hair and blue eyes and a magnificent figure; she was dressed with the simplicity of wealth with a sparkling bandbox finish that caused Adelaide to put an involuntary hand up to tidy away the curly wisps escaping from her cap. She was suddenly aware of the lemonade stains on her apron and its deplorably creased condition.

Margriet spoke. 'There you are, Coenraad. I wondered where you had got to.' She gave Adelaide a cursory glance. 'Are you coming?'

The professor had apparently not heard her.

'Sister Peters, I should like you to meet Freule Keizer.' He turned to the girl beside him. 'Margriet, Sister works with me in the clinic.'

The young women shook hands and smiled politely. Margriet's smile didn't quite reach her eyes.

'How awful for you, having to work.' She made it sound like an insult.

'But I enjoy it, you know,' Adelaide protested.

She was struggling to overcome her dislike of Margriet, who looked astonished and turned to the professor.

'You don't know how lucky you are. You've at last got a nurse who is wedded to her work.' Her tone made it clear that work was all that Adelaide could hope to wed. Her glance rested on Adelaide's hair and she allowed her beautiful eyebrows to arch slightly. She smiled. 'Such unusual hair! You must find it a great drawback.' The professor, listening idly, heard Margriet's last remark.

'How bad your English has become, Margriet. I don't think that drawback is the word you mean.' He sounded reproving.

Margriet laughed—she had a charming laugh.

'Do forgive me, Sister—there, I have forgotten your name already. It's quite true, my English is shocking; that's because I dislike speaking it, I suppose.' She turned to the professor. 'I must go and say goodbye to Lisette and Paula. Shall I wait for you in the car?' She didn't wait for him to reply, but said goodbye to Adelaide with cold charm, and slipped away.

'I must go too, Professor.' Adelaide looked pink and was breathing rather quickly, struggling to regain her temper.

The professor said, 'Of course, Sister, but don't forget that we shall all be meeting in my office in an hour's time to open our presents.'

When Adelaide got to the office it was just striking six o'clock. She was the last one to arrive and found Zuster Wilsma and the other nurses grouped around the desk, laughing and talking with the doctors.

The professor looked up as she came in. 'Good, now we can begin,' he cried, and pushed a pile of gaily coloured parcels in front of the youngest nurse. 'You first, Nurse Eisink.'

They all watched as she undid each parcel and admired the contents in turn. Zuster Steensma followed, her homely face alight with pleasure, and then Zuster Wilsma, and lastly Adelaide. As she unwrapped the first package she asked:

'But how can I thank the givers if I don't know who they are?'

Dr Beekman laughed. 'That's the whole idea, Sister. You mustn't know. Remember St Nicolaas gave them to you, and thank him.'

She did this, piling up the pretty trifles in front of her. The last two parcels were elegantly wrapped and tied with ribbons. She opened the flat box first, and gazed with delight at the fur-lined suede gloves inside.

'They're beautiful!' she exclaimed, and tried them on. They fitted perfectly. She looked around at the faces of the others watching her; it was impossible to tell from their expressions which of them had given her the gloves. 'Thank you, St

Nicolaas,' she said, and added, 'I can't think who they are from.'

She opened the last parcel. It was quite small, and she almost dropped it when she saw what it was, wondering who could possibly afford to give her Madame Rochas perfume. Perhaps all the staff had put together. She took a blissful sniff, and thanked the Saint with a fervour which left her audience in no doubt as to her delight.

The two men opened their parcels together amidst a good deal of laughing and joking from the nurses, and by the time they had finished it was almost seven o'clock. The doctors got ready to leave, Dr Beekman reminding Zuster Wilsma, who was on duty until the night staff came on, that he was on call. No sooner had they gone than Adelaide sent the two junior nurses off duty. They lived in Amsterdam, and were looking forward to an evening at home with their families, and more presents. Zuster Wilsma rammed the last of the paper and string into the wastepaper basket; she looked forlorn. Adelaide remembered that she lived in Amsterdam too.

'You live in Amsterdam, don't you, Staff Nurse? You go home too. I've nothing to do for the rest of the evening.' Her Dutch was clumsy, but Zuster Wilsma understood her and grinned with delight. She shook hands with Adelaide and tore off as fast as she could go. It seemed very quiet when she had gone. Adelaide sat down and looked at her presents again, wondering who had given them.

It was almost eight o'clock when she heard the ambulance bell. She went quickly to Casualty, switching on the powerful light over the couch and opening the door for the ambulance men. The blue flasher shone on the man hurrying towards her with a blanketed bundle in his arms. He laid his burden gently on the couch and took the blanket away. The little girl looked about two years old; she was unconscious, her little face the colour of skimmed milk. Even as Adelaide reached for the oxygen mask the blue tinge deepened, and the harsh breathing became more agonisingly difficult. Adelaide pushed an airway gently between the tiny teeth and slipped the catheter attached to the sucker down it. She switched on the motor, which made a reassuring purr. While she had been working, she had been aware of the mother standing close by. Now, with the essentials done, she turned to her. 'Bronchitis?' she asked. The woman nodded.

Adelaide beckoned to the ambulance man, glad he was one she had met several times before.

'You'll stay?' She pointed to the sucker and oxygen mask. He nodded and she went quickly to the phone on the desk and asked for Dr Beekman urgently. When she heard the voice on the other end of the line, she said in her quiet efficient voice:

'Dr Beekman? There's a small girl just in—bron-

chitis and laryngeal stridor. She's unconscious and
her respirations are very difficult. Will you come,
please?' The voice said 'Yes' as she put down the
phone and went back to the child, who looked
worse. She cleared the sucker, put it carefully down
the little throat again and gave it to the man to hold
again, then sat about laying up a trolley. The tracheotomy instruments were always kept ready;
there wasn't much for her to do. She drew up a
local anaesthetic into a syringe and was putting a
sandbag under the small shoulders when she heard
a car draw up outside. The ambulance man glanced
at her—he wanted to be on his way; she thanked
him as he hurried away, and said over her shoulder:

'The doctor is here. Everything's all right,' and
smiled reassuringly at the mother, sitting quietly in
a corner. She turned back to the child, who gave a
strangled breath as the professor came in.

He dropped his coat on the floor and stood for a
moment looking at the small convulsed face, his
fingers on the flaccid wrist.

Adelaide went to the head of the couch and
steadied the child's head between her hands.

'Everything's ready,' she said quietly. 'The local
is on the lower shelf.'

The child hadn't drawn another breath. The professor didn't stop to scrub, but quickly injected the
local anaesthetic, picked up a scalpel, and made a

cut—quite a small one—in the little throat, securing it with a small hook. He spoke softly to the mother—Adelaide thought it sounded comforting, although she couldn't understand what he had said—and the woman murmured a reply. He slit the trachea neatly, holding it open with the knife handle while he inserted the dilators. He mopped unhurriedly, and slipped in the tube with an unerring hand. He waited a moment, pushed the inner tube in and tied it securely. The operation had only taken a minute or two. They stood watching while a faint pink colour slowly started to blot out the blueness. The little girl's breath rasped in and out of the tube, but it was regular again. The professor dabbed at a tiny spot of blood on his cuff.

'Close call,' he observed. Adelaide's brown eyes smiled at him over her mask, and he smiled back. 'Nice work, Sister.'

He went to the phone and asked Zuster Zijlstra to come to Casualty as soon as she could. A moment later she came in quietly. She was a tall girl, with merry blue eyes; she and Adelaide got on well together. She winked at her now, and asked 'Busy?'

Adelaide, doing neat things with gauze and strapping, smiled.

'No, but you will be!'

The professor, who had been talking to the mother, turned round.

'Ah, my good Zuster Zijlstra, I want a cot, and oxygen tent, and a nurse to special this child. Will you fix them up for me, please?'

Zuster Zijlstra tossed her head. 'You always want something,' she complained. 'I'll do it at once, sir,' and disappeared again.

The professor walked over to the couch.

'I expect you've got some writing to do. I'll stay here.'

He stood by the patient, listening to Adelaide asking the mother the routine questions which had to be asked before the child could be admitted. She managed rather well, using a minimum of words and being very wary of the grammar. Her pronunciation was peculiar at times, but on the whole he thought that she must have worked quite hard during the month she had been in Holland.

Zuster Zijlstra came back. She scooped up the small figure on the couch very carefully and went to the door, which the professor held open for her.

'I'll come with you. I'd better write up some sedation and antibiotics for her.'

Adelaide finished what she was doing and showed the mother how to get to the ward, then began to clear up; there wasn't a great deal for her to do. She made up a fresh tracheotomy pack and put it in the autoclave, then stripped the linen off the couch and made it up anew. She was washing her hands at the sink when the professor returned.

'The child's fine. Zuster Zijlstra's a wonderful nurse.' He looked round. 'Where's Staff Nurse?'

Adelaide dried her hands carefully. 'At home. She lives in Amsterdam.'

'You took over her duty.' It was more of a statement than a question.

'Yes, sir. I don't mind in the least. I wasn't going anywhere.' She sounded quite cheerful about it.

'You should have taken your off-duty,' he said evenly.

She threw the paper towel in the bin, and went to turn off the autoclave.

'I rang Dr Beekman.' Her voice held a question, politely put.

The professor was getting into his coat.

'*Touché*, Sister Peters. I have taken Beekman's duty over until midnight; his people have come down from Drente for St Nicolaas.' He grinned at her, called good-night, and was gone.

## CHAPTER THREE

CARDBOARD Father Christmases had taken the place of St Nicolaas in the shops. Adelaide bought presents for her family and sent them home. She might have felt homesick, but the friends she had made among the hospital sisters took care to include her as much as possible in their own activities, so that she had little time for moping.

Mijnheer de Wit spent a whole lesson describing the Dutch annual holidays to her. It seemed that Christmas was strictly for the family and more sober than the English version. The giving of presents was usual in the larger towns; in the country the day was marked by a splendid meal and plenty to drink. Turkey and Christmas pudding hadn't gained much of a foothold, but many homes in Holland had a Christmas tree. New Year—now, that was different. The old man waxed eloquent in his beautiful Dutch—New Year was for everyone to enjoy. He made it sound exciting.

Adelaide had been rather puzzled by the amount of unwelcome attention her red hair had caused. Small boys called out after her in the street, mothers bringing their children to the clinic remarked on it, often with a laugh or pitying look. She was aware that her hair was rather unusual, but it had seldom been commented upon. One evening, at the end of a tedious lesson on the complexities of the Dutch verb, she mentioned it to her teacher. He broke into a rumbling laugh.

'My dear young lady, the Dutch, as a nation, dislike red hair, and your hair, if I may say so, is very red. You must expect comment upon it, at least when you are in public. I must add that this is the general opinion. Many people admire it,' he twinkled at her. 'I do myself.'

Dr Beekman was early the following day; he had some notes to write up, and sat doing this while Adelaide sorted the X-rays. They had become good friends and Adelaide had spent pleasant evenings with his wife Leen; the girls had liked each other at once. Adelaide put the last X-ray on the desk and turned to the doctor.

'Is my hair an awful colour?' she asked.

His blue eyes opened wide. 'Well, it is rather red,' he replied cautiously. 'Why do you ask?'

She started to tell him. She hadn't heard the professor come in; he leaned against the door, listening, as she explained about the small boys. 'Oh, well,' she said in a matter-of-fact voice, 'we're all afflicted with something, I suppose. Red hair is no worse than a squint or jug handle ears, or a large beaky n…' she stopped, because of the expression on Dr Beekman's face. He was looking over her shoulder, at someone behind her, and trying not to laugh.

The professor advanced into the room; his 'good morning' was quiet and uttered in a bland voice.

Adelaide felt herself blushing hotly, but she faced him bravely and said, 'I do beg your pardon, sir. I wasn't speaking of your nose...' she stopped and tried again. 'Yours is quite a nice sort...' She encountered the professor's eye. It was fixed steadily upon her; there was absolutely no expression on his face. She had a horrid suspicion that he might be laughing at her, and lifted her chin and looked down her own pretty little nose.

'I like beaky noses,' she said, and was relieved to see him smile.

'Thank you, Sister Peters. Your good opinion will do much towards enabling me to bear my affliction with equanimity.' He added thoughtfully, 'How thankful we should be that we do not have the squint.'

Adelaide smiled uncertainly. She still wasn't sure if he was amused or merely polite—as was his wont. She minded very much if he were to be angry; just lately she had found herself going to a great deal of trouble to please him...

The professor, however, did not seem to share her feelings. He was running through the X-rays on his desk, and said briskly: 'Shall we get started?'

He glanced at her, smiling faintly, and that was the only crumb of comfort she had.

Out-Patients closed for the two days of Christmas, but of course Casualty stayed open. Adelaide arranged to go on duty at one o'clock on Christmas Day, so that the nurses could go to their homes for the remainder of the day. She had been to the English Church in the Groenburgwal and sung carols, and felt a little homesick. There had been a dinner for the nurses on Christmas Eve; Matron had sat at the head of the long table, lighted by candles, and they had sung Dutch carols before they had started their meal. It had been pleasant and homely and she would write a long letter home about it.

It was very quiet in the clinic; Casualty was empty. She went along to her little office; she might as well start her letters, it would give her something to do. There was a parcel on her desk, wrapped in red paper patterned with robins, and tied with tinsel ribbon. Her name was on the label, written in the professor's deplorable writing. Inside were three books: she looked at the authors—Jan de Hartog, Johan Fabricius, and Charles Dickens. She was relieved to see that they were all in English as she laid them on the desk before her. It was nice to be remembered; probably the professor had thought that she would miss the presents she would have had had she been in England. He was, she noticed, very considerate towards his staff. She had read quite a lot of *A Christmas Carol* when the phone rang. She picked up the receiver quickly, expecting a casualty call; instead, she heard the professor's voice, sounding remote, wishing her a happy Christmas. She wished him one in return, and thanked him shyly for the books. She could hear a background of children laughing and shouting, and the steady murmur of voices, and pictured the family party gathered at his home; she supposed Freule Keizer was there too. Quite unbidden, a large lump came into her throat; she swallowed it desperately back and said in a steady voice: 'I'm wanted on the other phone, sir. Goodbye.'

After a minute or two she pulled herself together, chided herself for being such a spiritless goose, and went into the tiny clinic kitchen to make herself a cup of tea.

Two days after Christmas, the clinic opened again, and as was to be expected, it was packed. The waiting room was full to overflowing by nine o'clock, and Adelaide, feverishly hunting for notes and X-rays, hoped that they would get finished by first dinner. Punctual to the minute, the professor, accompanied by Piet Beekman, stalked in. He wished her good morning briskly and added briefly in a deceptively mild voice: 'As fast as you like, Sister. I hope all the notes and X-rays are here; we have a full morning's work.'

Adelaide stiffened with resentment at the unfairness of his remark. She wasn't a conceited girl, but she was aware that she did her work well. She shot him a cross look, wasted on his downbent head.

Staff Nurse Wilsma, back from a well-earned coffee break, had brought Adelaide's post with her. She took it gratefully, glancing at the envelopes before stuffing them behind her apron bib. One of them had an Amsterdam postmark. She wondered what it could be, but there was no time to look. Zuster Steensma was struggling in with a small boy who was screaming and kicking and hitting at her with his small fists. His mother scuttled in after them; she looked frightened as she dodged round them and took the chair in front of the desk. The professor looked up from his notes and smiled at her, but forbore to speak; he would not have been heard in the din.

Adelaide handed Piet the examination tray she was holding and sailed across the room like a pocket battleship, plucked the small tyrant from the wilting nurse, and whisked him on to a couch. Admonishing him soundly for being such a bad boy, she removed his shoes and top clothes with the ease of long practice, evading his arms and legs with skill. He was so astonished that he stopped crying, and when he opened his mouth to start again, Adelaide pulled such a face that he burst out laughing instead.

'Now be quiet,' said Adelaide. She had discovered that the children responded just as well to English as Dutch; it was the tone of voice that mattered. There was quiet in the room. The professor murmured something to Dr Beekman, who laughed. They came over to the couch together, and Piet smiled at her and patted her on the shoulder.

'It must be that hair of yours, Adelaide!'

While they were drinking their coffee, she remembered her letters; there was no time to read them all, but she glanced at the two from England, then opened the Dutch one. The envelope was large and of very thick paper. There was an invitation inside from the professor's aunt, for Old Year's Night. She couldn't understand quite all of it, and took it over to the professor.

'My aunt,' he said. 'She has a party every year, and always invites my clinic Sister.' He frowned at Piet's astonished face, and not giving him the chance to speak, said, 'You and Leen are going, aren't you, Piet? You could take Sister along with you, couldn't you?'

'Yes, of course.' He turned to Adelaide. 'You'll love it, it's like Christmas and St Nicolaas rolled into one.'

That evening, he told Leen about it. 'There's never been a clinic Sister invited to his aunt's house before.'

His wife laughed. 'But, Piet, remember that Adelaide is a stranger here—I expect Coenraad thinks she deserves some fun while she's in Holland.'

Adelaide was ready and waiting when the Beekmans called for her. She had taken great care with her hair, the chestnut brown bow she wore in it exactly matched her velvet dress. It was last year's, but it suited her anyway. She hadn't been able to afford a new one. It was a bitter cold night, and they were thankful for the fragrant warmth which enveloped them as Bundle, the butler, ushered them into the hall of the Baroness's house. A maid took the girls upstairs while Bundle took Piet's coat and went in search of the professor, who followed him back into the hall.

'Piet, before we begin the festivities, that case we admitted today...' the two men became absorbed. Adelaide, coming downstairs with Leen, had ample opportunity of studying the professor in the hall below. She hadn't seen him in a dinner jacket before; he looked very handsome. Her heart began to beat faster; he had never seen her out of uniform. The two men turned round, and the professor's eyes swept over her and on to Leen. She doubted if he had even noticed that she wasn't wearing her cap and apron. She said good evening in a small voice, and they all went into the salon where his aunt was standing. She greeted Adelaide pleasantly, and beckoned to Mijnheer de Wit, who was standing nearby, and asked him to take her

round and introduce her to everyone. Adelaide
went with him from group to group, murmuring her
name as she had been taught, and trying to remember the names murmured back to her. Her hand was
shaken so many times her arm began to ache. The
old gentleman drew her on one side.

'Now you know everyone, Miss Peters.'

Adelaide shook her head. 'I can't remember a
single face or name.'

He laughed, and patted her arm. 'Never mind,
here's someone you know anyway.' He nodded towards the professor, who was crossing the room.
Margriet Keizer was with him; she had an arm in
his, and was chattering gaily. She looked charming,
her green dress making Adelaide very aware of her
own slightly out-of-date model. The head-to-heels
glance Margriet gave her as they shook hands did
nothing to improve Adelaide's feelings, and she
suddenly wished with all her heart that she had
never come. She glanced around her; she just didn't
belong, these people were so obviously well-to-do
and leisured and beautifully gowned. The thought
that they might be pitying her, as Margriet was,
pinkened her cheeks. She hated the professor's aunt
for inviting her; she hated him too, just because he
was there, carelessly friendly and not in the least
interested in her.

They stood together in a small group, while she
matched Margriet's gaiety with a wholly false vi-

vacity of her own. This put a strain on her usually retiring nature, and when a young man in a brocade waistcoat joined the group and asked her to dance, she accepted with pleasure. She didn't much care for the owner of the waistcoat, who was, she suspected, younger than herself, but at least he wanted to dance with her. The professor had had ample opportunity to do the same if he had wished. She sensibly decided to enjoy herself. Her partner danced well, their steps suited, they circled the large room, and she took care to turn a smiling face in the professor's direction. It was a pity that he wasn't looking. He was dancing with Margriet.

During the next hour or so she had frequent glimpses of him; she noted that he danced with a great number of the women guests, and several times with Margriet. She was agreeably surprised to find that she did not lack for partners, and danced every dance, telling herself sensibly that she might as well forget the professor. Having come to this conclusion, she went off to the supper room with Jan Hein, the youthful owner of the brocade waistcoat, and lingered over the delicacies provided until almost midnight. When they went back to the salon everyone was standing, glasses in hands, waiting for the clock to strike. Its silvery chimes were drowned by the outburst of sirens and hooters and fireworks from all over the city. Glasses were raised and a round of hand-shaking and kissing began.

Adelaide, unused to the tonic effects of champagne, was enjoying herself; she had even forgotten the professor, standing talking to his aunt, just behind her. She watched Jan pushing his way towards her through the crowd, and realised that he was rather drunk. She decided to evade him, and stepped backwards into the professor's arms. She felt herself turned neatly round to face him, to be kissed squarely on her mouth.

'A Happy New Year, Miss Peters.' The band had just started to play again, a Strauss waltz, and before she realised what was happening, they were half way round the room.

'How very high-handed,' she remarked coldly.

He reversed neatly into a corner. 'Don't you like dancing with me, Miss Peters?'

She looked up at him, and said with an incurable honestly. 'Yes, I do, very much.'

They went on dancing; she hoped that the band would forget to stop and tried to think of something clever to say. Her mind was blank, but luckily the professor didn't appear to be much of a conversationalist while he danced. She stopped worrying and gave herself up to the pleasure of dancing; the professor danced very well indeed, but she had known he would. The music stopped and someone tapped her on the arm. It was Piet Beekman.

'We must go, Adelaide. The baby-sitter said one o'clock, and not a moment later. Are you coming?'

Before she could reply the professor said in his easy way:

'Why not let Sister stay? I am sure she will have no lack of offers to see her home, and in the unlikelihood of her being on her own, one of us will see her back later.'

'Thank you, professor, but I should like to go now; I'm on duty in the morning.' She spoke quietly in a stiff little voice and turned away with a brief good night to find the Baroness, who rather surprisingly kissed her and urged her to come and see her again. Adelaide made a vague reply to this, thinking it very unlikely that she would see her hostess again. She intended to concentrate on her Dutch lessons and her own small circle of friends in the hospital. She watched the professor and Margriet going towards the balcony. She wasn't sure what she had expected from this evening— perhaps that if he saw her out of uniform, he would realise that she was a girl as well as a highly trained cog in the hospital machinery. As she went upstairs with Leen to get her coat, she allowed herself to remember that he had kissed her, but then so had a great many other people; she derived little comfort from the thought.

She said goodbye to Leen and Piet at the door of the Sisters' home, and went upstairs to her room, where, despite the lateness of the hour, she sat on her bed thinking about the evening. One fact emerged very clearly—she was in love with the professor.

She had a whole day to get over the party. Casualty was slack; there was no clinic. She sat in her office, scowling over her Dutch grammar. After a while she shut her books and wrote a letter home. She gave a colourful and gay account of the party; it was slightly exaggerated, as she wanted her family to know what a good time she was having. She carefully made out a money order to go with the letter. The boys' school fees would be due again soon. They were clever, and deserved the best ed-ucation that could be managed. Her thoughts played truant again, and she wondered if Professor Van Essen was rich. She had no idea where he lived, but she supposed he had a good practice in Amsterdam. It was natural that she should think about Margriet Keizer too, for she was obviously a close friend of his.

Adelaide opened her book again; she was behav-ing like a silly schoolgirl. She reminded herself what she was doing and who she was. She resolved to think no more of the professor, but work for him to the best of her ability and be pleasant and friendly and take no interest at all in his private life. She was well aware that this high-minded resolve, if put to the test, might well prove worthless; in the meantime, she told herself sternly, she would apply herself to her Dutch grammar.

The day seemed endless—Wilsma took over Casualty duty at two o'clock, and Adelaide went out into the grey cold day and walked until she was tired. The streets were almost empty; she supposed that everyone was within doors, visiting or receiving visits from family. She began to feel lonely, but told herself resolutely not to give way to self-pity, and when she found a small café open went in and had a cup of coffee, and walked back to the hospital again. Most of the Sisters were out, and supper was quickly eaten by the few who remained. She went to her room and busied herself washing her hair, until Zuster Zijlastra came in to tell her about her visit to her home. It was late when she finally put out the light, to lie awake in the dark, remembering the professor's kiss and their dance together. Common sense reminded her that nearly everyone in the room had kissed her too—he had only done what was obviously the custom. No amount of wishful thinking on her part could make it otherwise. She went to sleep on the hopeless thought.

She felt nervous at the idea of seeing the professor again, but she need not have worried. There was no time for talk beyond a hurried good morning. Casualty was full with children who had burnt themselves with fireworks, eaten too much, or, taking advantage of the relaxing of parental discipline over the holidays, had found the matches and got burned, or sampled the contents of aspirin bottles. Adelaide stayed in Casualty, while Zuster Wilsma took the clinic, and the professor and Dr Beekman went back and forth as they were needed. By mid-day Casualty was empty again, and they all sighed with relief. It was fortunate that the morning clinic had been a small one. Refreshed by their one o'clock dinner, the staff assembled once more for the afternoon session, which Adelaide knew would run far over the scheduled time. There was little leisure for private thought, which was perhaps why she was able to work cheerfully with the professor for the rest of the busy day without any feeling of awkwardness or embarrassment. By the end of the afternoon she had slipped back into their usual professional friendliness—casual and matter-of-fact, and quite impersonal. It had been easier than she had expected.

A few days later the professor mentioned that he had some beds at another hospital in Amsterdam. 'Only four,' he explained, 'to take the overflow if we get a run on the beds here. I'll arrange for you to be taken there one day, so that you can look around.'

Adelaide was packing dressing drums with a practised hand.

'I should like that, sir, thank you. If you could give me two or three days' notice so that I can arrange the duty rota.'

She snapped a lid shut, opened the perforated strip around the drum, and put it on to the loaded trolley.

The professor scrawled his signature, put away his pen, and got up to go.

'Very well, Sister. I'll let you know. Good night.' He walked to the door, but stopped halfway and said over his shoulder: 'Are you quite happy here, Sister Peters?'

Adelaide folded a dressing towel, flattened it with a thump, and laid it with its fellows.

'Yes, sir, I am, very.'

He gave a non-committal grunt and went out, leaving her standing staring at the closed door, wondering wistfully if he minded in the least if she was happy or not.

The promised visit to the hospital took place at the end of the week, but not, as she had hoped, in the professor's company. Dr Beekman took her in his Volkswagen. It was a bitterly cold day, with low grey clouds, turning yellow at the corners.

'Snow,' said Piet Beekman. 'A good thing we arranged to come today.'

Adelaide braced herself against the seat as he raced round a corner, much too fast.

'Doesn't the professor come to see his patients?'

Dr Beekman cut a swathe through a bunch of
dignified cyclists, miraculously missing them all.

'Yes, more often than not—but he's going to
some reception or other at the Amstel Hotel early
this evening, so he wanted to get away in time.'

He drew up with a squeal of brakes, wrenched
the wheel round, and shot up a side street, to stop
with devastating suddenness before a large gloomy
door.

'Here we are,' he said cheerfully, and leant over
and opened the door for her to get out. Adelaide
took stock of her surroundings. The hospital was
on a corner, and looked bleak. Once inside, however, she discovered that the bleakness outside had
not been allowed to penetrate its walls. The wards
were bright with coloured paint and gay with flow-
ering plants; the children in them looked happy.
The place sounded like a parrot house. Half way
round, Dr Beekman was called to the phone. She
guessed what it was before he told her. He had to
go back to the clinic.

'I don't suppose I shall be long,' he said. 'One
of the Sisters will take you round the rest of the
wards and I'll come back for you later.'

'No, don't come back, Dr Beekman, I'm sure I
can find my way back. Just tell me the number of
the tram I have to catch, and I can't go wrong. And
if I do, I'll get a taxi.'

He was uncertain. 'Are you sure?' He thought for a moment. 'You'll need a twenty-four tram.'

Adelaide nodded. 'I'm off duty at five o'clock, anyway. I'll go straight to the Home.'

He looked relieved. 'All right, then. See you in the morning. *Tot ziens.*'

Another hour sped by. Theatre Sister, who had taken Piet Beekman's place, insisted on Adelaide having a cup of tea before she left. They sat sipping the weak, milkless beverage, carrying on a halting but entirely satisfactory conversation. It was nearly six o'clock when she got up to go. Assuring her kind hostess that she could get back to her own hospital quite easily, she went down to the entrance hall. There was no one about, so she opened the heavy door and stepped out into the street. It clanged shut behind her, a second before she made an instinctive movement to push it open again. She was standing in a blizzard; she had never been in one before, but this blinding curtain of snow couldn't be anything else.

Adelaide stood hesitating, glad that she had worn a raincoat and boots. She looked around as well as she was able; there was no one to be seen, and no traffic either, but she guessed it would start again as soon as the snow stopped. She decided against going back into the hospital. She would walk in the direction of the trams, and wait until they started again, or even take a taxi. She began to walk along the street, taking the right-hand fork as Dr Beekman had said. The snow was already thick under her feet, but by keeping to the wall by the side of the street, she made quite good progress. The bridge was a surprise—she didn't remember it—it looked a temporary affair, and she walked carefully over it and followed the wall curving to the right. Through the snow she caught the glint of water, and stood still, trying to remember where she was. It didn't take long for her to realise that she was, for the moment at least, lost.

Luckily she hadn't come far; she decided to retrace her steps to the hospital and shelter there until the weather cleared or someone could take her back. Halfway over the bridge, she glimpsed a large brick building looming ahead; it looked like a brewery or factory of some sort. It had been on her left as she approached the first time. At least, she thought so. She realised, suddenly, that she didn't know any more. She stopped, clutching the flimsy handrail, swallowing panic, and forcing herself to look carefully in all directions. The snow, beating into her face, half blinded her, nevertheless, she decided, with a sudden lifting of her spirits, that there were lights on her left, and not too far away. Where there were lights, there would probably be people. She walked slowly towards them, terrified that she would lose them. She picked her way through the snow, the lights becoming blessedly stronger with each step. They came from a large building, streaming from glass doors at the top of a flight of steps.

Adelaide climbed, aware of the icy wetness of her feet in her sodden boots. There was a uniformed man at the door, who opened it for her, and she stood on the doormat in front of him, oblivious of his startled look, brushing the snow from her face so that she could see where she was. She was in a large, luxurious foyer, lights from half a dozen chandeliers shone on gleaming tables and mirrors and massed flowers. A group of men, immaculate in white ties and tails, were talking some yards from her. Adelaide had time to recognise the professor before he looked round and saw her, and walked across the thick-piled carpet towards her. He looked distinguished and elegant and very angry.

'What in thunder are you doing here, Miss Peters?' His habitual calm seemed to have deserted him completely.

If she hadn't been so cold, she would have burst into tears; as it was, she said as clearly as her chattering teeth would allow:

'I'm lost. I came in to ask the way.' She frowned as fiercely as her snow-stiffened eyebrows would allow. 'I had no idea you were here,' she added with a monumental dignity rendered pathetic by her grotesque appearance. 'Please don't let me keep you from your friends. The doorman will explain how I can get back.'

The professor, with a resigned air, said nothing, but unbuttoned her raincoat and took it off. He said something briefly to the doorman, who disappeared and returned within the minute with a pair of slippers, which he substituted for Adelaide's useless boots.

'Won't you take off your hood, Miss Peters?' The professor spoke with excessive politeness. She obeyed wordlessly, and watched her clothes borne away out of sight.

'They'll be dried,' he explained briefly. 'There's a writing room here, you can wait there. It will be empty at this time of day.'

She scuffled after him in the too large slippers. As they passed his friends he murmured something, and they smiled at her and nodded with kindly faces, so that she smiled shyly back at them. The writing room was small and cosy, with a small fire burning cheerfully. The professor indicated a chair which he had drawn up to its warmth. 'I'll get someone to bring you some coffee.' He gave her a nod and disappeared.

The coffee was hot, and tasted rather peculiar but nice. Adelaide drank one cup quickly, and poured a second cup from the elegant pot. There was a small plate of tiny sandwiches on the tray; she tried one. She hadn't tasted anything like it before and she didn't know what it was, but found it delicious. She drank the rest of her coffee and felt a pleasant warm glow spreading over her; she supposed it was the warmth of the little room which made her feel so sleepy. She ate another sandwich, then closed her eyes. When she opened them again, the professor, looking remote, was sitting in a chair opposite hers. She sat up at once, and said in her matter-of-fact voice:

'I went to sleep, it was so warm in here. If my coat's dry, I'd like to go, please. I expect the snow has stopped by now.' She got up, very conscious of her untidy hair and crumpled skirt. The professor got up too.

'I'll ask them for your things and arrange for you to go back.' He walked to the door, but before he could open it, it was flung wide, and Margriet Keizer came in. She looked magnificent, in a low-cut gown that showed off her figure to perfection. She ignored Adelaide and spoke rapidly and angrily in Dutch to the professor. He chose to ignore her ill-humour, and answered placidly in English.

'Ah, Margriet, you had my message. Miss Peters got lost in the snow on her way back to hospital. Fortunately she came here for help. I'm just going to arrange for her to go back. Perhaps you'll keep her company while I'm gone.'

He left them together, standing in hostile silence. Margriet rustled to a chair.

'How stupid of you to go out in such a bad snow-storm, Miss Peters. I suppose it was chance that brought you here?'

Adelaide looked surprised. 'Yes, of course it was chance, Juffrouw Keizer. I had no reason to come here otherwise.'

'Well, it was an unfortunate chance for us. Do you realise that we are guests at a reception here and that I have been left alone without an escort while Coen—Professor Van Essen wastes what should have been a pleasant evening?'

Adelaide flushed hotly. 'If your evening has been spoiled, I'm sorry.' She paused and looked at her watch, surprised to see that it was after seven. 'It is still early, and you have the evening before you.' She spoke quietly, genuinely sorry for the other girl's disappointment. But her sympathy was wasted.

'It's not much use being sorry, is it, now that the harm's done. You don't seem a very sensible young woman. It seems to me that you can't be very suitable for your job.'

Margriet broke off as the professor came back into the room with Adelaide's things. She thanked him for them in a tight little voice and put them on quickly, evading his helping hand. She said good night to Margriet, who made no reply, and went across the foyer, not noticing the people in it. The professor caught her up at the door.

'Not so fast, Miss Peters. I need my coat.'

Adelaide was pulling on her gloves, her nice warm gloves St Nicolaas had given her.

'I am perfectly able to go home, sir. Thank you for your help, and I'm sorry if I've spoilt your evening.'

The words came out in a rush, rather louder than she had intended. He looked at her reprovingly.

'I shall take you back to the hospital, Miss Peters. You are one of my staff and I am responsible for you. Kindly say no more.'

He shrugged himself into his coat and took his gloves from the doorman. They went outside together, the snow had stopped falling—it had already been swept away from the hotel steps. The Volvo crunched with gentle disdain for the soft, treacherous stuff through the quiet streets. There wasn't much traffic about, but the tramlines were already being cleared. The professor turned the car and headed it towards the centre of the city.

'Forgive my curiosity, but why did you allow yourself to get caught in the bad weather? It must have been snowing...?'

She explained. It sounded rather silly.

'I should have gone back inside and waited. It was foolish of me. I've given you a great deal of trouble...'

'Yes, indeed you have,' agreed the professor. After that, she could think of nothing further to say.

When he stopped outside the Sisters' Home, he said merely: 'Stay where you are,' and got out and walked round the car and opened the door. The snow had piled up; he didn't seem to notice that it was covering his thin evening shoes. He leaned down and whisked her out of her seat and over the drift, on to the doorstep, and set her gently on her feet. He rang the bell.

'You are a goose, aren't you?'

His voice was the calm one he used on his more contrary patients. Adelaide blinked, her eyes suspiciously bright. He wasn't angry, he wasn't even annoyed. He had not, in fact, wasted any feelings on her at all. She said good night in a subdued voice and went inside, where she met Zuster Zijlstra coming out of the sitting room. The big girl looked at her with astonishment.

'Adelaide, where have you been?' Her big blue eyes explored her friend's deplorable state.

'I got caught in the snow-storm.' Adelaide spoke gaily. 'I want a bath and a huge meal.'

They went laughing upstairs together, and at supper Adelaide, using the mixture of English and Dutch the other Sisters managed to understand, gave them all an amusing and not quite accurate account of her evening.

It didn't seem so funny when she was in bed. She looked at her watch. For the professor the night would still be young. She pictured him at the

Amstel Hotel, dancing, she supposed, with Freule
Keizer. She remembered his thin shoes in the snow,
and went suddenly to sleep half way through an
improbably day-dream in which he had contracted
pneumonia from wet feet, and she had saved his
life by her devoted nursing.

The professor showed no signs of pneumonia the
following morning, however. He came into the
clinic, looking in the best of health, at exactly nine
o'clock. There was a nurse off sick, and he had to
wait until Adelaide and Nurse Eisink fetched the
first two children. Adelaide settled a tired-looking
woman into the chair by the professor's desk, and
started to peel off the numerous woolly garments
of the very young baby she had brought in. The
professor put down the out-patient card he was
reading.

'Someone off sick, Sister?'

She paused in the process of unbuttoning. 'Zuster Steensma, sir. She caught cold yesterday.'

He put the card down.

'Zuster Steensma does not appear to enjoy your
iron constitution, Sister Peters.'

Adelaide disentangled the rest of the baby from
its clothes, rolled it neatly in a blanket and gave it
back to its mother. She glanced towards the desk,
and he gave her a friendly smile.

'And an iron constitution is one of the least of your many attributes.'

She blushed. He must have overhead Margriet on the previous evening. The day, which had begun rather badly, suddenly took a turn for the better.

## CHAPTER FOUR

TOWARDS the end of January the weather became very cold. Frost sparkled everywhere and the canals were covered with ice. Within three days, the first skaters appeared. The nurses hurried off duty in anoraks and slacks, their skates slung around their necks, making for the nearest canal. The skating went on until after dark when lights shone across the ice, hot chestnut and potato chip stalls sprang up like magic and did a roaring trade. The Dutch were enjoying one of their favourite sports.

Casualty became crowded with children with cracked collar bones and wrists and ankles. The nurses recounted tales of their prowess on the ice to Adelaide; they were all anxious that she should learn to skate. It was so easy, they explained; all you needed was a strong skater to hold you up while you found your feet and got your balance. They suggested several people who might teach her, but warned her jokingly not to accept any offer of help from Professor Van Essen; he was an expert on skates who, while tolerant of beginners, didn't care to waste his time on them. Dr Beekman, who had come in while they were chattering, agreed that the professor was very good indeed, and he couldn't imagine him wanting to teach anyone.

Adelaide could think of nothing she would like better than to be taught to skate by the professor, but it was obvious that if she were to wait for him to offer to do so, she was unlikely to set foot on the ice at all. It was unfortunate that the professor should choose that morning to ask her if she had been on the ice yet. She replied, 'No, sir,' in a most uncompromising manner, and when he further suggested that she should join him with Piet and Leen on the ice that evening, she put down the tray of instruments she was carrying with a quite unnecessary clatter.

'It's very kind of you to ask me, sir, but I...' she hesitated, for the professor was staring at her thoughtfully, and searched desperately for an excuse, wishing at the same time that she could stop blushing like a silly girl whenever he spoke to her. Her sigh of relief was quite audible when at length he said:

'Another time, perhaps, Sister Peters?'

He said no more, and she went along to Casualty with her tray. When she returned shortly afterwards, he had gone to do a ward round.

She wished that she had told him that she was unable to skate; but if she had done so, she reflected, he was too kind a man to do other than offer to teach her, and that, as the nurses had said, would never do. The sight of a group of rosy-cheeked nurses, on the way to the canals, and glowing with well-being, did nothing to improve her mood, so that when she met two of the housemen from the main hospital on her way over to lunch, and they invited her to skate with them that evening, she accepted with alacrity. She didn't know them well; she wasn't even sure she liked them, but she wanted to skate. The thought that once she had learned she could accept any further invitation from the professor overcame any doubts she had as to whether she really wanted to go out with Dr Visser and Dr Monck. They promised to bring some skates for her, and arranged to meet her after eight o'clock that evening. She ate a hurried lunch, worrying about what she would wear. She finally decided to go shopping, and came back with blue slacks and an anorak which fastened tightly under her chin. She went back on duty quite excited, longing for the evening.

Adelaide enjoyed her first lesson on the ice. She found it exhilarating, and her vague feeling of dislike for Doctors Visser and Monck was lessened by the delight of finding herself on skates. They held her up while she got her balance, and then went slowly up and down the canal with her between them. She was awkward at first, but by the time they had gone the length of the canal three or four times she was beginning to find her feet, although she had to keep her eyes on her skates, which had a habit of going the wrong way if she didn't. Doctors Visser and Monck carried on a conversation over her down-bent head, pausing from time to time to beg her to keep her feet straight, strike out strongly with the left foot, and above all, keep her head up.

Adelaide obediently lifted her eyes from her all-important feet, clutched her companions firmly and looked around her. The Singel was crowded; the children had gone, their places taken by older girls and boys, married couples skating arm-in-arm, courting couples with arms entwined around waists, and elderly gentlemen showing a surprising turn of speed. The Singel was well lighted, and she saw the professor while he was still some distance away. She realised that he had seen them too, for he was making an apparently leisurely progress towards them. He had his hands clasped behind his back, and looked, just as most of the men she had seen that evening, very much at home on his skates. He came to a quiet halt and gave her a cold stare.

'Good evening, Miss Peters. Enjoying yourself, I trust?'

Adelaide smiled at him. 'Yes, thank you, very much.'

He nodded casually to her companions. 'Your— friends are giving you a good time?'

'Oh, but they're not my friends,' she spoke with

devastating candour. 'I've said hallo to them in hospital, of course, but I met them this afternoon and they said they would teach me to skate.' She smiled at them in turn and then at the professor, who, however, did not smile back. She remembered guiltily and very clearly then how she had refused his invitation to join his skating party that evening. How ill-mannered and rude he must think her—her pink cheeks grew scarlet and she opened her mouth to explain just as Piet and Leen, closely followed by Margriet, joined them. Leen asked her if she was all right and she said, 'Yes, thank you. I'm doing awfully well—I hope.'

Margriet laughed softly. 'How clever of you to find two men to teach you, Sister, and don't you feel foolish learning to do something you would normally learn as a child?'

Adelaide was unable to think of anything to say to this remark. She turned to Dr Visser.

'Please may we go on skating? I don't want to miss a minute.' She smiled at everyone, taking care to include Margriet, who said at once: 'Don't let us keep you. Go and enjoy yourself—I'm sure you will with these two young men.'

There was a sly note of amusement in her voice which made Adelaide uneasy. She forgot it a moment later, however, as they left the others behind and continued on their way. She was doing better now, striking out boldly and much too intent on keeping her balance to do more than wonder what Doctors Visser and Monck were arguing about. They turned and went back along the other side of the canal. Half way down they passed Piet and Leen who waved, and then the professor and Margriet, who did not. Adelaide, watching them skim past, had to admit to herself that although she liked skating, she didn't much like being with her two companions.

'I'd like to go back,' she said suddenly, and was surprised when they agreed to do so without demur. They all climbed the bank and took off their skates and set off in the direction of the hospital. They walked together, arm-in-arm, and Adelaide, grateful for their kindness, kept up a steady flow of conversation in her halting Dutch. They had been walking for ten minutes or more before she realised that they weren't going in the direction of the hospital.

'You've taken the wrong turning, I'm sure; the hospital's over that way.' She pointed over her shoulder. Dr Monck laughed, and gave her arm a tug.

'This is another way back—besides, there's a club here, just down the street. We'll have a drink and a bit of fun.'

Adelaide frowned in the dark. 'I don't want a drink, thank you. You both go to your club and I'll go back.'

She had no idea where she was now, but that didn't matter. Dr Monck held her arm a little tighter.

'Don't be a silly girl, of course you'll have a drink—several drinks.'

Adelaide didn't like the way he laughed. She stood still, planting her feet firmly on the icy road, and disengaged her arms from their too friendly grasp. She sought vainly for the right words in Dutch, but could think of none. She would have to use English and hope that they understood.

'I'm not being unfriendly,' she said crisply, 'but I don't want a drink. Thank you,' she added politely. 'I'm going back to the hospital.' She once more removed their arms; they were laughing again, standing close on either side. She drew a deep steadying breath.

'If you don't leave me alone I—I shall plant you a facer!'

The professor's quiet voice, suggesting that the two young men should take themselves off, while he saw Sister Peters back to the hospital, fell into the ensuing silence like drops of icy water. Doctors Visser and Monck stood looking sheepish and foolish. Adelaide gave the professor a relieved smile and then turned to the two young men.

'Thank you very much for teaching me to skate, and I hope you have a pleasant evening at your club.'

They mumbled a reply as she turned away and started to walk back the way she had come, this time with the professor at her side. After a while he broke the silence.

'Do you know what a facer is, Miss Peters?'

Adelaide was surprised at such a silly question; she had two young brothers at home.

'Yes, of course I do, sir.'

'And would you have—er—planted them?'

She nodded. 'Don't you think I could?'

'On the contrary, Miss Peters,' his voice was dry, 'I'm sure that you are capable of anything.'

They walked on in silence until they arrived at the hospital gates, where they paused.

'I must explain something.' Adelaide spoke in a determined voice. The professor eyed her.

'Don't bother,' he advised. But she was not to be put off, and started to speak, the words tumbling over each other.

'I was told that you were a very good skater, and hadn't much patience with beginners, so I couldn't go with you, could I? But I didn't want to tell you—I was going to learn first, so that if you asked me again... And then I met those doctors. I don't know them very well, and I don't think I like them very much either, but they said they would teach me to skate.' She looked at him shyly, and added with her usual candour: 'I'd much rather have been with you, but you do see that I had to learn to skate first, don't you?'

She was standing under the lamp at the hospital gates; it shone on her hair, which had escaped from her hood. It glowed like bronze in the light. She looked about fifteen years old, and very pretty.

'Didn't anyone tell you that those two young men were rather wild?' She shook her head. 'No, I don't think so, but my Dutch isn't very good yet, someone may have told me and perhaps I didn't understand.' She looked apologetic.

'I shouldn't go out with them again, if I were you,' advised the professor. 'Wait until you can hold your own in our language.'

'That's a very good idea, sir. I'll take your advice. It was kind of you to bring me home,' she continued. 'How fortunate that you happened to be coming down that street just then.'

The professor agreed.

'I wasn't frightened, you know, but it was rather unpleasant. Thank you very much, and good night, sir.'

She went indoors and up to her room to undress and lie in bed and remember every word the professor had said; and that, she decided, as she prepared to sleep, was easily done, for he had said very few. On his way home, the professor called in at the Beekmans' flat. They had just got in, and Leen was making coffee. He took off his coat and accepted the cup she offered him, then told then what had happened.

'Are you skating tomorrow evening? You are? Good, Piet, will you invite Adelaide to go with you, and I'll meet you on the Koningsgracht about seven. Between us we should be able to turn her into a passable skater, but don't tell her that I'm coming too; she has a bee in her bonnet about attaining perfection before accepting any invitation to skate with me. The silly girl,' he added.

Leen poured out another cup of coffee.

'Let's all come back here afterwards; though I haven't anyone to sit with little Piet.' She frowned.

Coenraad got up and put on his coat.

'Mrs Tweedle will love to come; I'll ask her.' He thanked Leen for the coffee, wished them both good night, and went home.

Adelaide was delighted when Piet asked her to go skating with them that evening.

'I'd love to, if you're sure I won't be a nuisance?' she asked anxiously. 'I'm not awfully good yet.'

'You're doing very well,' Piet said stoutly. 'Another few hours and you'll be as good as any of us—well, almost as good.'

She found Leen and Piet waiting for her. It was already dark, but the ice on the canals glistened in the lights. There were more skaters than ever. They started off, Adelaide in the middle, still rather uncertain of her feet. They had not gone far when Leen cried:

'Look who's here! Coenraad, how nice to see you!'

He came to a halt beside them. He was wearing a sheepskin jacket and his dark hair was uncovered; he was going grey at the temples and it showed up under the lights. He slapped Piet on the shoulder and kissed Leen's cheek. The little nod he gave Adelaide was friendly, she wondered why he looked so pleased with himself. She looked around, but there was no sign of Margriet.

'I'll get between you two girls,' he said, and crossed his arms and took Adelaide's hand in his gloved one.

'Which foot?' she asked anxiously, and they all laughed, and he gave her hand an encouraging squeeze.

'The left.'

Two hours later they all sat down on the bank and took off their skates. It had been wonderful. Adelaide had stopped looking at her feet once she had realised that the professor would not let her fall. It was a great deal more fun now that she was able to look around her. She told him so, turning her glowing face to his. She looked very happy. They were all panting and very hungry; their breath wreathed around them in little clouds; it would be very cold later on in the night. She sat down and let the professor untie the knots she had made in her straps. Their faces were very close, her dark eyes sparkled as she said:

'I could have gone on for ever. I felt so safe with you.'

The professor took off her skates and tied them together. 'Your skating does you credit, Miss Peters, you will soon be safe on your own, won't she, Piet?'

He took off his own skates, picked up Adelaide's, and they all set out, in the best of spirits, for Piet's home.

The flat was warm and cosy when they reached it. A nice-looking elderly woman was putting on her hat and coat as they came in. Leen introduced her as Mrs Tweedle who had been minding the baby. She gave Adelaide a bright bird-like glance as the professor escorted her politely from the room. While they were waiting for the taxi, he said:

'Thank you, Mrs Tweedle, I'll be back in a couple of hours. Don't wait up.'

'All right, Mr Coenraad.' She got into the taxi and settled herself comfortably while he gave his address to the driver. He stood back, and she put her head out of the window.

'That's a nice young lady, that new nurse of yours, sir. Nice manner too,' she breathed.

He agreed. 'And an excellent addition to our staff, Mrs Tweedle, a pity that she will only be with us for a year.'

They had an uproarious supper. Leen thought it would be a good idea if Adelaide spoke Dutch. This she was very willing to do; she had quite a large stock of words by now and had learnt a great deal of grammar. Her efforts at conversation, however, though determined, provoked so much laughter that they decided that it might be better to speak English. After supper the girls cleared away the dishes and washed up in the tiny, well-equipped kitchen, and Leen went to fetch little Piet for his bottle. She gave him to Adelaide to hold while she went to get it ready. He was a big placid baby, and sat on her lap, his head pressed against her shoulder. Adelaide stroked the soft blonde down on top of his head; she had quite forgotten the two men sitting on either side of the stove, talking quietly; little Piet smelled nice and gurgled sleepily and chuckled when she tickled him. It must be nice to have a baby, she thought wistfully.

The professor took her back to the hospital soon afterwards. The roads were ice-covered and slippery. He took her arm and walked with a rocklike steadiness down the middle of the street, hoisting her gently back on to her feet each time she slipped. For most of the way they walked in a companionable silence. When they did talk it was about the

next day's clinic, and the hospital and the chance
of the ice holding for a few more days. When they
reached the hospital gates Adelaide said in her
friendly voice: 'Wasn't it a lovely evening? I'm so
glad I can skate. Thank you for teaching me.' She
wished him good night and watched him go back
through the swing doors into the quiet streets. She
still had no idea where he lived, and wondered if
she would ever know him well enough to ask. She
thought it unlikely.

Adelaide was late off duty. Now that she was thoroughly settled into the clinics she scrubbed for theatre if there were emergency ops. There had been
three that day, all within an hour or two of each
other. There had been a prodigious clearing-up to
do afterwards. She changed quickly, wrapped herself well against the raw cold of the evening, and
walked quickly to Mijnheer de Wit's flat in the
Spui. She was beginning to enjoy her Dutch lessons; she could understand a fair amount of what
was being said by now, although she was still hesitant about talking. However, her teacher seemed
pleased enough with her, to judge by the amount
of homework he gave her. He was waiting for her
now in his untidy little sitting room and she has-
tened to make her apologies. He listened gravely,
correcting her accent as she spoke, and making her
repeat her words again, until she was perfect. She

took off her outdoor clothes and spread her books
on the table.

'You are a good pupil, Miss Peters,' he said in
his dry old voice.

Adelaide was surprised. 'Am I? How kind of you
to say so,' and she added with candour: 'It's a terrible language.'

The old gentleman laughed. 'Now you know
why so many of us speak English and French and
German, even if only a few words. But you have
tried very hard, and I will reward you a little. We
will shut the grammar and we will talk. You may
ask questions of me—in Dutch, of course—and I
will answer them.'

Adelaide, who hated grammar in any language,
shut her books and settled back in her chair. She
looked charming, her hair gleamed like copper in
the light, she was wearing a dark green dress,
which was the envy of her colleagues, who had not
got the advantages of Marks and Spencer. There
were a great many things she wanted to know, and
one thing in particular.

'Why does Professor Van Essen wear glasses?'

Mijnheer de Wit took off his own spectacles and
looked at her sharply.

'Miss Peters, I find that a most peculiar question.'

'Yes, I know, but I don't mean to be impertinent.
You see, it isn't just curiosity. I've noticed he

doesn't use one of his eyes…' She added apologetically, 'I work with him every day, and I look at him quite often.' She went a little pink.

Mijnheer de Wit put his glasses back on. 'You are a perceptive young lady. Coenraad van Essen is practically blind in one eye, but it is never mentioned, you understand?'

Adelaide sat forward. 'Please tell me about it; you must know that I like and admire him…'

Her teacher nodded vaguely. 'It's quite a story—we will have a cup of coffee before I begin.'

Their cup of coffee had become a small ritual which Adelaide knew better than to ignore. She got the cups and saucers and silver rat-tail spoons and put them on the table, while the old man fetched the coffee. He poured it carefully, put some Speculaas on a plate of Pynacher Delft at Adelaide's elbow, then settled himself in his chair.

'Coenraad's father was a great friend of mine. He was an excellent and well-known doctor, not a children's specialist, as his son is, but a physician. When the Occupation took place in 1940, he was left alone by the Moffen and allowed to carry on with his work. Coenraad and his two sisters were small children, you understand, and I don't suppose the war meant a great deal to them at that time. Not until their father was arrested for helping his Jewish patients to escape. He was shot, his house and possessions confiscated, and his wife sent to a

camp. Coenraad's mother died there. You have perhaps heard of the Tweedles, who look after
Coenraad?' Adelaide nodded. 'They went into hiding when the doctor was shot and his wife arrested
and took Coenraad and the two little girls with
them. They cared for the children until the
Bevrijding, and later went back to the house on the
Heerengracht with them. They are devoted to
Coenraad, and he to them. It was a considerable
time after the children were back in their old home
when Coenraad confessed that he was gradually
losing the sight of one eye. He had been knocked
about quite considerably when his parents were arrested and the house searched; a blow from a rifle
butt had damaged his eye; by the time he could be
taken to a specialist, there was nothing more to be
done about it.' The old man looked across the table
to Adelaide. 'You haven't drunk my excellent coffee.'

She had forgotten all about her coffee. She was
still seeing a small boy—nine, ten years old?—being ill-treated by brutish adults. She raised enormous brown eyes, suspiciously bright, to her
teacher.

'He is always so kind and patient with the children. That's why, of course.'

Mijnheer de Wit made no comment, but said
again:

'Drink your coffee, and we will have a second cup.'

She drank, swallowing the chilly liquid without tasting it. He filled their cups and she took a sip and went on speaking her thoughts out loud.

'He seems so…self-sufficient. Doesn't he want to marry?'

He didn't seem surprised at her question.

'When Coenraad decides to marry, I think it unlikely that he will tell anyone about it beforehand.' He paused, and added slowly:

'There are always rumours, of course.'

Adelaide blushed. 'I didn't mean to be inquisitive—he's such a nice person, I would like him to be happy. He deserves it.'

Her teacher sucked the last of the sugar from his cup, making a regrettable noise in doing so.

'He will be…he will be. Now, my dear young lady, let us discuss your homework. You still have great difficulty with the conditional; supposing you study it well before your next lesson, and we will try and overcome your reluctance to speak in any tense but the present.'

Adelaide gave a little laugh. 'I'll do my best, Mijnheer de Wit. You are so kind and patient, I only hope that when I am back in England I'll have an opportunity to speak Dutch. It won't be very likely.'

She got up, took the cups out to the tiny kitchen,

and put on her coat. She had said good night, and was half way down the precipitous little staircase to the floor below when the front door bell jangled through the house. She heard the click of the lock as it was opened by the kind of remote control commonly used in the older houses. Someone was coming upstairs, two at a time, and very fast. She had time to clutch the narrow hand rail firmly before the professor was upon her; he filled the staircase completely.

'Don't knock me down,' she cried, and then, 'Good evening, sir.'

He had stopped on the stair below her. 'Good evening, Miss Peters.' He cocked a black eyebrow at her books. 'Lessons?' He didn't wait for her to nod. 'Will you wait for me? I want to talk to you. I have to give this to De Wit.' He indicated the pile of papers under one arm. 'I'll only be a moment.' He edged past her and went on up, not waiting for her reply.

She continued on her way, and sat down on the bottom step to wait for him. He was back again, empty-handed, after only a few minutes, and opened the door and ushered her outside. There was an icy wind blowing down the Spui as they turned into the Kalverstraat, walking briskly. When they reached the narrow steeg which was the accepted short cut to the hospital, he kept straight on. Adelaide hesitated, not sure if she was supposed to turn down its familiar gloom, but he took her arm and steered her past and across the street to the warm, well lighted lounge of the Hotel Polen. Adelaide sat down on the chair he had pulled out for her, trying to think of something to say. She very much wanted to ask him about that awful time when his parents were arrested, but was fairly certain that if she did so, he would simply not answer, but get up and go away and leave her alone. So instead she made a banal remark about the weather, which he ignored. He ordered coffee, and at last broke the silence.

'I won't keep you long, Adelaide, but it's too cold to stand talking in the street.' He unfastened his coat and told her to do the same. It was richly warm in the café; she hoped that he would put her heightened colour down to the fact that she was feeling the change of temperature. The coffee arrived, and he sat back in his chair, looking away from her out of the window, so that she could watch him unobserved. She jumped when he spoke.

'What is your opinion of Nurse Wilsma?'

Adelaide took her eyes off his face and thought.

'May I ask why you want to know before I tell you, sir?'

'You may. When you go back to England, we shall have to appoint a new Sister in your place. Nurse Wilsma seems an obvious choice, but I—we don't see every aspect of a nurse's work, you know. She's good, but she is also...' he frowned, trying to find the exact word he wanted '...slap-dash, though not always.'

Adelaide put down her cup; she didn't really want it, it was a good excuse not to have to drink it.

'She's very good, especially in an emergency—and sweet with the children, and that's important to you, isn't it? Perhaps she is a little slapdash, but she is young, isn't she? Give her a few months as a *Hoofdzuster*, and you will find she is everything you could wish for.' She pushed her cup away, and in a quite different voice said:

'I don't go back to England until October. It's still only March...unless you wanted me to go back sooner?'

He was thunderstruck.

'Good heavens, no, Miss Peters. The thought never entered our heads. We are more than pleased with you.' He shot her a sharp glance. 'I thought you knew that.' He smiled at her, and looked all at once ten years younger. 'Did you think that I was giving you the sack?' he asked mildly.

She smiled back at him. 'No, not really, but you did sound as if you couldn't wait for me to leave.'

'Forgive me, that wasn't my intention. Now, about Nurse Wilsma, could you prepare a monthly report—I do not need to say an honest one, to you.

That will give us several months to assess her before we offer her the post.'

Adelaide started to do up her coat.

'Yes, of course I will, Professor, and I'm sure that they will be excellent ones, too. And now you won't mind if I go?' She got up, and he got up with her. 'I've kept you, I'm sorry.' They were at the door. 'I'll say good night, sir.'

'Say whatever you like, Adelaide, but perhaps you will bear my company as far as the hospital? I want to look in on that fractured pelvis you had in theatre this afternoon.'

They crossed the street and started to walk down the *steeg*. It had begun to rain.

'A pity it won't freeze any more now,' the professor remarked. 'I enjoyed our skating party, didn't you?'

'Yes, very much.' Adelaide smiled up at him, thinking for the hundredth time what a nice person he was to be with, and they fell to arguing in friendly fashion about the Dutch weather. The walk to the hospital had never been so short for her as it was that evening.

# CHAPTER FIVE

ADELAIDE was standing, hot and rather tired, drying instruments. It had been a very busy day. Casualty had been more than usually active. Only swift action had saved the life of a two-year-old toddler with extensive scalds, and that had meant delays in dealing with all the many and various injuries that came in. Adelaide had somehow managed to be in two places at once, helping in Casualty and supervising Out-Patients for Dr Beekman, but the professor had become more and more demanding, so that in the end she had had to stay with him. They worked together over the child, setting up a transfusion of blood plasma, going swiftly through the whole routine of shock treatment, meeting each emergency with the seemingly unhurried movements of experts. When at last the small patient was carried carefully to the ward, the professor had followed it, leaving her to deal with the minor ailments still waiting.

The last one dealt with, she looked at the clock. Out-Patients would have finished some time ago. Adelaide started cleaning up. She had had no tea, and only a snatched dinner, so that when the professor strolled through the door, looking cool and immaculate and presumably without a care in the world, she threw him a look over the mask she had not bothered to take off which caused him to raise an enquiring eyebrow.

'You've had no tea, Sister,' he stated sapiently.

She gave a little snort behind her mask, and went on stringing forceps with the ease of long practice. He came nearer.

'You look like an enraged bundle of calico,' he remarked cheerfully, eyeing the enveloping theatre gown. Only her muslin cap, perched on top of her rather untidy hair, looked fresh and dainty. He leaned across the trolley and twitched the mask down under her chin. She gave an exasperated gasp, but he took no notice, removed the forceps from her grasp and continued stringing them. He handed her the completed bunch.

'You put them away, you know where they go far better than I.' He cast an eye over the trolley. 'You've done the needles and knives? Good, we shall be ready in ten minutes or so.' He handed her another bunch. 'I've not had any tea either,' he said, in such a plaintive voice that she burst out laughing.

'But the Dutch don't mind missing their tea in the afternoons, it's only the English who can't bear to go without it.'

The professor nodded. 'I know, I had an English

grandmother and an English nanny. Between them they taught me a proper respect for afternoon tea.'

Adelaide shut the cupboard door and locked it. 'So that is why your English is so good, Professor?'

'Thank you. I imagine your Dutch will be equally good if you continue to make the progress Mijnheer de Wit tells me about.' Adelaide looked surprised, and he went on to explain. 'He was a friend of my father's, and naturally he assumed that as you are working at the clinic, I should want to know how you are getting on.'

Adelaide undid her gown and put it with the pile of sheets and dressing towels ready for the laundry. She glanced up at his words, to find him staring at her intently. She felt a quick glow of excitement, instantly dispelled by his next remark.

'You look hot and tired,' he observed.

Adelaide sighed.

'Yes,' she agreed, 'I am.' What he really means, she thought, is that I'm bedraggled and bad-tempered; and I am. She stripped off her frills, rolled down her sleeves, and put on her cuffs.

The professor looked at her watch. 'Since I have been the cause of you missing your tea, perhaps you will come and have a meal with me in—shall we say—forty minutes? I'll be at the hospital entrance.'

Adelaide, half way through the door, stood with her mouth open, looking at him. Her eyes looked

enormous, her lipstick worn off hours ago, the end
of her nose shone, and she was quite unaware of
how pretty she looked despite it all. She shut her
mouth with a snap.

'It's very kind of you, Professor Van Essen, but
I have other plans for the evening.' She spoke
stiffly; she was a poor liar and avoided looking at
him.

'What plans?' he persisted. She searched feverishly for a genuine excuse, failed, and looked at
him helplessly. He met her embarrassed gaze
blandly.

'Just so, Sister. You don't consider it quite—
suitable for a member of the nursing staff to accept
an invitation from a consultant; but I must really
point out to you that you have been with us for
some time now, and I have had no opportunity of
talking to you about your job and reactions to
working here in Amsterdam. Since we're both hungry, surely we can—how do they say it?—kill two
birds with one stone?'

Adelaide, listening to him skilfully cutting the
ground from beneath her feet, wished most unreasonably that he had asked her for any other reason
than that of convenience. She remembered what
Mijnheer de Wit had said about her hair. Perhaps
the professor wouldn't care to go out with someone
as conspicuous as she was.

'What about my hair?' she said gruffly, and watched him look her over, rather taken aback.

'I imagine you will run a comb through it,' he suggested mildly.

'I don't mean that.' She stopped and swallowed. 'You don't mind going out with it?'

The professor suppressed a smile. 'No, I don't mind. Should I?'

'The Dutch don't like red hair, and—and people stare at me sometimes. Mijnheer de Wit told me. You heard me telling Piet Beekman about it.' She went rather pink.

'I remember. We discussed ears and noses too, didn't we?' He spoke seriously enough, but she cast him a suspicious look.

'Yes, well, you know what I mean. Do you mind?'

'No, I don't mind. You forget that I had an English grandmother, perhaps that accounts for the fact that I quite like it.'

Adelaide felt relieved. 'Then I should like to come, thank you. I'll be at the front door in about half an hour.'

She whisked away, all her splendid resolves forgotten in the excitement of going out with the professor.

She looked very nice as she came down the hospital steps, thirty minutes later. Her green coat was well cut, and the little green hat matched it exactly;

she was wearing the gloves that St Nicolaas had given her. She greeted the professor rather shyly, but with great composure. She had taken herself to task while she changed. The professor was a kind and considerate man for whom she worked and as such it was perfectly natural that he should take an interest in her work. It was all very simple. Just the same, when she had taken a final look in her mirror she had turned away quickly, suddenly pierced with a longing to be blonde and Dutch and beautifully dressed, and, above all, admired by Coenraad van Essen.

She looked about her with naïve pleasure as she got into the professor's dark green car, and re-marked with a disarming frankness:

'How beautifully it's polished. Whenever do you find the time to keep it all so?'

The professor made a little choked sound and thought of Henk, his elderly chauffeur, who cher-ished the car like a baby, not to mention the Rolls-Royce in the garage behind his house. He tried to imagine Henk's face if ever he found his master cleaning the car.

'I have some help,' he said briefly. 'Do you drive, Miss Peters?'

'Oh, yes,' said Adelaide cheerfully. 'My father's got an old Austin, but I'm a bad driver, and as we can't afford a car for a good many years yet, I only drive when there's no one else.'

They turned into the Leidsestraat and, after a minute or so, pulled up. 'Here we are,' said the professor. 'I thought at first we would go the Five Flies, but I think you'll like it better here.'

She looked at the sign over the door. Dikker and Thijs. She had never heard of them. They went inside to a quiet, elegant opulence that took her breath. There was music somewhere in the background as the head waiter came forward to greet them.

'*Goeden Avond, Juffrouw,*' he bowed smilingly to Adelaide.

'*Goeden Avond*, Mijnheer de Baron.' He led them to a table and settled her in a chair. She looked across the table, frowning quite fiercely at the professor, who waved aside the proffered menu, and sat back comfortably, waiting for the question he knew was coming.

'Why did he call you Baron?'

'I am.'

'You mean that you're a baron as well as a professor? I didn't know.' She sounded disapproving.

'Yes,' he answered coolly. 'I saw no reason to tell you.'

She looked like a little girl who had been unexpectedly slapped.

'I'm sorry, Adelaide, I didn't mean that. I inherited one and worked for the other. It doesn't make any difference, you know. I'm the same man I was ten minutes ago.' He beckoned the hovering waiter. 'Would you like to choose, or will you leave it to me?'

She looked at the menu; it was large and listed an impressive array of dishes. It was written in Dutch too. She might choose something fearfully expensive.

'Please will you choose for me? Something simple,' she added, mindful of his pocket. The professor chose carefully, ordering dishes which would have cost her a week's pay. The waiter went away. Adelaide clasped her hands in her lap, and said in a little rush:

'I'm sorry, Professor.' She sounded rather stiff, but eyed him honestly. 'I was very rude. Of course it's none of my business. It's just that I was surprised.'

She had no idea what a peculiar effect she was creating on her companion, but privately and fervently wished that she could stop blushing.

'Thank you, Miss Peters. Tell me, don't you approve of titles?'

She opened her eyes wide. 'Well, of course I do. Only I'm not used—that is, I don't know anyone with one. I—I don't come from that sort of background. My father's a country parson.' She said it with pride.

He smiled charmingly. 'Yes, I know, your Matron told me. Tell me about your family.'

She didn't realise how skilfully he was putting her at her ease. It wasn't until they were sitting over their coffee that she said suddenly:

'You wanted to ask me questions about my work, and I've talked and talked.' She looked at him anxiously. 'Did I bore you?'

'Indeed no, I've enjoyed every minute. We can talk about work some other time.'

'I think I should go back now,' she said. She hadn't realised that they had been sitting there for so long. He didn't try to stop her.

'Supposing we drive back round the canals?' he suggested. 'It's a lovely evening. Amsterdam is at her best on these spring nights.'

The professor knew his own city well, pointing out the picturesque houses and telling her small fragments of history which he thought might interest her. Half way down the heerengracht he stopped the car. 'Shall we get out for a minute? You'll see it all so much better, and it's very lovely here.'

It was indeed lovely; the canal lay smooth and cold in the moonlight, and on either side the beautiful gabled houses stood as they had stood for centuries. Adelaide had a strange feeling of timelessness. She sighed and shivered. The professor put an avuncular arm around her and pulled her close into the comfort of his tweed coat.

'You're cold. I shouldn't have suggested that we got out of the car.'

'I'm not cold; it's just that this is all so beautiful and peaceful and ageless. I shall miss it very much when I go back to England.' She pointed across the canal. 'What a lovely house that is, opposite. I wonder who lives there, and if they love it and look after it. I expect it's beautiful inside.'

'Yes, it is.'

'Have you been inside?' she asked.

'I live there.'

Adelaide turned to look up into his face.

'You mean you live there…it's your home?'

'Yes. It's rather large for me, you know.' He smiled down at her. 'The ancestor who built it had a wife and children; I shall have to follow his example.'

Adelaide didn't reply. The idea of the professor having a wife and children and living happily with them in his lovely house, while she went back to England and never saw him again, was very lowering to her spirits. She wanted this moment to last for ever; his arm felt very solid and comforting around her, and she would have liked to have buried her face in his shoulder and had a good cry. Instead, she took a few steadying breaths.

'It really is time I went back.' Her voice didn't sound quite right, but she persevered. 'Thank you for a delightful evening. I did enjoy it.'

She moved, but instead of releasing her, his arm tightened and pulled her round to face him. He put a finger under her chin and tilted her face up to study it intently. She looked white in the moonlight, and forlorn. She stood passive in his arms while he bent his head and kissed her; she returned his kiss with an innocent passion, forgetful of everything but that moment. When they drew apart she whispered:

'Please don't say anything.'

They got into the car, and drove without speaking to the hospital. The professor helped her out and went and pulled the old-fashioned bell outside the nurses' home, then stood waiting beside her on the doorstep. He was as calm and self-possessed as usual. She stole a look at his face; it was impossible to read his thoughts. He turned his head and looked at her in a detached, faintly amused way. She thought wearily, 'He was just being kind.' She said in her soft little voice:

'Thank you for comforting me just now—I suppose I was feeling homesick. I'll not think of it again, and I know you won't wish to either.' The door opened then, and she slipped inside with a murmured good night.

The days slipped by; it was the end of spring, although the weather was still cold, with rain and wind and low-flying clouds. Adelaide did some sight-seeing. She went to Alkmaar—the cheese market wasn't open, it was too early in the year, but she loved the quaint little town. She explored Delft, and wandered round its magnificent churches and longed for enough money to buy some of its exquisite pottery. She spent a day with one of the Sisters whose home was in Medemblik. It was like living in the sixteenth century again, only the inhabitants spoilt it by wearing modern clothes. She whiled away several hours in the old castle; it was cold and draughty and grim, but it had a lovely view over the Ijsselmeer.

The clinic was as busy as always; in Casualty, burns and scalds and injuries from skating gave place to broken arms and legs from falling off bicycles, and limp little people who had fallen into the canals, fishing or sailing boats.

That particular Saturday there had only been a small clinic in the morning. Dr Beekman had taken it as the professor was away. Casualty was slack too. Adelaide sat in her office and worked at her books and thought about him. She supposed he was somewhere with that odious Freule Keizer. She got out a sheet of paper and applied herself to making out the off-duty for the following week. She sat and looked at it for a few minutes, then tossed it aside rather pettishly and began to draw rows of beaky noses on her blotting pad. She wondered what Zuster Boot had meant when she said that the professor came from a patrician family. She would look it up when she went off duty. On second thoughts, she decided that she wouldn't look anything up; she was getting far too interested in the man. She tore up the beaky noses and started once more on the off-duty. She decided, once again, that she would be pleasant and friendly in a cool way; she was a sensible young woman, not a silly girl, it should be quite easy to keep to her resolution. She drew a splendid beaky nose, with eyes beside it adorned with glasses. She looked at it longingly, then tore the paper up savagely.

That evening she went for a long walk with two of the Sisters. They got back to the home tired out, and she went to bed and slept at once. She was awakened by one of the night Sisters, and sat up in bed to find the light on. She looked at her clock. She had only been asleep for half an hour; it was barely eleven. Night Sister came from Friesland, and spoke a Dutch Adelaide found difficult to understand, but she was able to make out that there had been a bad accident—a bus full of children coming home from a school outing. There were, according to first reports, a lot of casualties; she was wanted on duty at once.

Adelaide dressed fast, screwed her hair up anyhow, and pinned her cap on to the deplorable result. She fastened her blue buckled belt as she ran: she had forgotten her cuffs. All the lights were on in Casualty and the clinic; one of the nurses was already laying out extra equipment. Adelaide swept

instruments off shelves, collected receivers and
trays, and put them in the autoclave. She told the
nurse to lay up trolleys wherever she could find the
room, and asked her to get the salines and blood
plasma bottles out, then she went to the cupboard
and got out the two satchels which were kept for
emergencies; she was collecting the pethidine and
morphia ampoules from the DDA cupboard when
Piet Beekman came in. He saw the satchels.

'Good girl, we'll go straight there. They can
manage here for the time being. There'll be plenty
for us to do.'

They caught up their satchels and ran outside to
the waiting ambulance. It raced through the city,
along the Rokin, across the Dam Square and into
Damrak, and turned off into one of the small streets
close to the station. It halted on the edge of a large
crowd, which made way for them to reach the
space cleared by the police. The small victims were
lying and sitting around the wreckage from which
the police and ambulance men were still passing
children. The bus in which the children had been
travelling had gone into the back of a lorry-load of
scrap-iron, and an oil tanker behind it, unable to
stop in time, had hit the bus with such force that
the back had been lifted high into the air. It now
rested at a sharp angle, its nose buried in the piles
of scrap-iron on the wrecked lorry, its back wheels
in the air.

They wasted no time: Dr Beekman marshalled his helpers into a team, and started going from one child to the next, Adelaide with him, giving the necessary injections and first aid so that the children could be moved as soon as possible back to the hospital. Two ambulances had already moved off; Adelaide and Piet were bending over a small boy when a policeman made his way over to them. He looked worried. 'There's a child still in there,' he said. 'She's jammed on the steering wheel and none of us can reach her. We're waiting for the acetylene cutters and the other equipment; the fire brigade are bringing them, but it will take a bit of time to clear the nose of the bus from the wreck of the lorry, before we can use any of it. The child's injured for sure, and terrified. We're afraid she might fall before we can get her out, and there's nothing but broken glass and iron below her.'

Piet said, without pausing in his work: 'Isn't there enough room for a man to get through, or are you afraid of his weight tipping the bus?'

'Both,' said the policeman. 'We've had several attempts.'

Adelaide finished a neat bandage on the boy's leg and got up from her knees.

'Let me go,' she said. 'I'm small and light enough to crawl down the bus, and I'll stay with the child until you can get us out.'

Piet looked doubtful, but she gave him no time

to say anything, and walked quickly across to the
wrecked bus with the policeman. He picked her up
and lifted her until she could reach the ruined door,
get a hold on it, and wriggle inside. She was appalled at the mess; it was a shambles. She kept very
still and looked round her, deciding what to do. She
would have to make her way down the steeply in-
clined bus to where she could hear the child crying.
She began to edge through the mass of broken seats
and woodwork. As she got nearer, her torch picked
out the terrifying barrier of broken glass between
her and the child. Great spears of it stood rooted in
the floor, hideous icicles of it hung from the crazy
ceiling. Adelaide crawled nearer; she could see the
little girl now, covered in dust and filth, and frantic
with fear. She was on her back, her body wedged
in the spokes of the wheel, her head hanging and
small legs dangling. Adelaide went as near as she
dared, slid an arm carefully between two jagged
pieces of glass, and put it under the child's head.
Then she eased the other arm through a splintered
hole and under the thin small knees. She drew a
sighing breath and took stock of the situation. The
child, as far as she could see, was covered in
scratches and abrasions, but there did not appear to
be any large wound. She was light in Adelaide's
arms, but they were already starting to ache, and
she wondered how long she would be able to sup-
port the small body, crouching awkwardly, not dar-

ing to move. She was conscious of a fine dust creeping up her nostrils; her clothes were covered in it. She had lost her cap; her hair hung in a red tangle around her shoulders, her apron was hopelessly torn, and so was the sleeve of her dress. She supposed that help would come soon. The little girl looked at her with enormous eyes; she had stopped crying. Adelaide smiled.

'Hullo, what's your name?'

She could barely hear the whisper: 'I'm Miep.'

'What a lovely name,' said Adelaide chattily. 'Well, Miep, I'm going to sit here with you for a minute or two until someone comes to get us out. Shall I tell you a story?'

She embarked on a story of The Three bears. It was a jumbled mixture of Dutch and English; she wondered if Miep had any idea what it was about— she wasn't sure herself after a minute or two, but it seemed to soothe the child, for she didn't cry again. Only when a piece of wreckage came tumbling wildly down the bus, to slide away into the dark around them, did she cry out. Adelaide's voice faltered as the torch beside her toppled over and rolled away, its light doused. She cried in a frightened little voice, 'Oh, Coenraad, please come.' Saying his name had made her feel better; she suddenly knew that he would, and told Miep so in such a cheerful voice that the little girl stopped crying again and listened quietly to Adelaide's story.

\*    \*    \*

Coenraad van Essen sat beside his aunt in the stalls
of the Concertgebouw; the programme of classical
music was almost over, but to the professor the
strains of Beethoven's fifth symphony merely provided a dimly heard background music to his
thoughts. His mind was wholly engaged with the
problematic treatment of the acute interssusception
which he had admitted that afternoon. He was annoyed to be disturbed by a tap on the shoulder. He
listened to the whispered message given to him by
an attendant, spoke briefly to his aunt, and went to
the manager's office to take Dr Beekman's call. He
listened without interrupting while Piet spoke, said
briefly that he would be along at once, and went to
get his car.

He drove fast through the city, passing ambulances with lights flashing, on their way back to the
hospital. Obviously the rescue work was well under
way. He parked the car in a side street, and pushed
his way through the crowd. He saw Piet immediately kneeling beside a little girl. Coenraad looked
round. There weren't many children left, those that
were didn't appear to be badly hurt. A fire tender
drew up beside the wrecked bus, and several men
began to unload equipment. He'd got to Piet by
then, and without more ado held the small skinny
arm flexed while Piet arranged a sling and gave him
a short and concise account of the children's injuries and what had been done for them. An ambu-

lance man arrived and carried the small patient away and they moved on to a boy, sitting propped up against a pile of coats. Blood trickled sluggishly down his face from a scalp wound, it had dyed his shirt a dark, sticky red. Coenraad laid him down with the observation that surely everyone knew that head cases lay flat. His skilful fingers were probing the long cut hidden under the blonde hair. 'He's a concussion all right. Get him back to the clinic, Piet, as soon as possible.' He was busy with a pad and bandage, and frowned suddenly.

'I thought you said Adelaide was with you? Has she gone back?'

Piet looked up. 'No. There's a child trapped in the nose of the bus, she's in there with her.'

The professor said nothing, but looked at the up-ended bus and turned to Piet with raised eyebrows.

'There wasn't anyone small or light enough to get to the child.'

Coenraad nodded. 'I see. But I think it's time I got them out.' He went over to the men standing round the fire tender and stood talking for a minute, then took off his dinner jacket and hoisted himself through the door Adelaide had entered. It was very dark inside, but he could hear Adelaide's voice. He listened carefully to the queer jumble of words and grinned to himself. It was then that his foot touched a piece of the wreckage, which went slithering down towards the nose of the bus. The child cried out in the sudden silence which followed. He heard Adelaide call too, but it seemed wisest not to answer her.

When he got back to the rescue squad they had already begun to cut a hole through to the driver's cabin; they had moved as much of the scrap-iron as they dared, and now two men stood ready with a metal stretcher from one of the ambulances. As the cut metal fell away they eased it through on to the mass of glass and splintered wood inside. It would make a firm base from which to work. The professor lowered himself to the ground and wormed his way carefully inside the bus.

Adelaide, crouching by the now unconscious child, saw the light from his torch and had a brief shadowy sight of him, and then heard his quiet voice.

'Adelaide? Are you all right?'

'Coenraad! Yes, I'm fine.' She tried hard to stop her voice from shaking. 'I think Miep is unconscious; she hasn't answered me for the last few minutes.'

The professor was quite close to her now, separated by the smashed glass. He glanced at her briefly.

'Keep still for a little longer.'

She watched while he got cautiously to his knees and examined Miep. It was a good thing that the small creature had passed out; he would be able to work much faster. He ran gentle hands over the flaccid arms and legs; he could feel no broken bones, it was more likely that there was an internal injury. The wheel was wrapped around her waist, gripping her fast. He set to work on it, while Adelaide tried to keep her arms from shaking; the strain on them was almost unbearable.

It seemed a long time before Miep was free and he was able to take her in his arms and lower himself on to the stretcher again, to push her carefully out to the waiting hands beyond. He knelt down again and took the glass cutter from his pocket. Adelaide had pulled her arms back, and crouched, resting them on her lap. Their numbness was giving place to a cramp which was almost unbearable, and bringing her near to tears. When the professor after one fleeting glance, asked 'Cramp?' it was all she could do to nod—she would not trust her trembling mouth to form the words.

He spoke bracingly. 'Rub your arms and try and move your fingers; you'll need them in a minute to plait that hair.'

This time she managed a shaky smile and said in a determinedly bright voice: 'Very well, I'll do my best.' He wasn't looking at her now, so she could let the tears trickle down her dirty cheeks; it was surprising how much better she felt for them. She rubbed her arms as she had been bidden to do, the professor was lifting away the first pieces of jagged glass as she started, very clumsily, to gather her hair into a plait. There was very little room; she dared not move too much, it took a long time; by the time she had finished he was easing away the last splintered sheet of glass between them.

He was so close to her that she could see the little beads of sweat on his forehead. The same fine white dust that coated her face was on his; his hair was powdered with it too. She dismissed the frivolous thought that he would be a remarkably handsome old man with the speed it deserved, and worried instead about the long scratch she could see on the back of one of his hands. Her alarming thoughts of tetanus and a possible dreadful death were brought to an abrupt end by the professor's voice, very much alive, its placid tones unaltered by his recent exertions.

'Put your arms around my neck, I'm going to lift you through.' She felt his arms around her waist, and clasped her own round his neck, and was lifted neatly through the hole he had made. His deep, rather pedantic voice was just above her ear.

'You have a saying in English—It's an ill wind that blows nobody any good.'

'Whatever do you mean? I don't see…' They were kneeling on the stretcher now, and she loosened her hands from his neck and looked enquiringly at him in the torchlight. She was quite unprepared for the quick light kiss he gave her. He laughed a little.

'Now do you see? This is my honorarium.' Without another word he pushed her down on to the stretcher and towards the gap where they were waiting to help her out. Piet helped her to her feet and gave her a bear-like hug.

'Adelaide, are you OK?'

'Yes, of course. What about the little girl, is she all right?'

'She's in hospital by now; she looked pretty bad, but at least she's alive.'

He gave her a warm smile and turned to grin delightedly at Coenraad. The glare of a flash lamp made them start; there were several more as they joined the firemen and police, busy clearing up the mess. After a few minutes they said goodbye, and Adelaide found herself between the two doctors, being hurried to the car. They put her between them on the front seat, and the professor turned the car towards the hospital. He spoke briefly to Piet over her head.

'Rub Adelaide's hands, will you, she's going to need them presently.'

It was pleasant to sit back while Piet massaged her tingling hands in his great paws, and watch the professor, as relaxed as though he were returning from an evening's outing, shoot the Volvo between two trams, with a broad grin for the indignation earthily voiced by the drivers. To his enquiry, presently made, as to how she felt, she answered briefly:

'I'm fine, thank you.'

'You're filthy dirty.' He barely glanced at her. She wondered what she looked like, and was glad there was no mirror for her to see. The professor was speaking again in a brisk voice.

'Half an hour for us all to have a bath and change. Sooner, if you can manage it.'

He swung the car through the hospital gates and stopped outside the Sister's Home. Lights were on in Casualty and the theatre wing, the clinic was ablaze with them. Adelaide found herself lifted down and propelled gently to the door, which the professor opened for her. 'Thank you, sir,' she said politely, and was surprised when he took one of her very dirty hands in his and said:

'You're a very brave girl.' His voice sounded kind. He gave her a little push and went on in a different, brisk voice: 'Half an hour, not a minute more.'

It wanted five minutes to the half hour when Adelaide arrived at the clinic. Excepting for her hair, which she hadn't had the time to wash, she looked exactly the same as usual. She put on a gown and tied her hair in a theatre cap, then pushed open the door of the Intensive Care room. Piet was already there and looked up as she went in.

'Hullo, Adelaide. There are three for theatre here. The fractures are already over on Orthopaedic, the rest are warded here. The professor wants you in theatre to scrub up. Dr Van Hoven is operating, they're going to be tricky cases.'

There were plenty of nurses on duty, the hospital hummed with them. The theatre was ready and waiting for the first case. Adelaide scrubbed up and started threading needles and checking swabs. The doors opened and the first patient was wheeled in, the anaesthetist at the trolley's head. The child was put on the theatre table. It was just after one o'clock in the morning.

The last case was wheeled out of theatre at half past four. Dr Van Hoven stripped off his gloves, and he and the anaesthetist, nodding their thanks to Adelaide, went off together. She started to clean the knives and needles while the two nurses washed and sorted instruments and cleaned the theatre. They were all tired, but no one disputed the rule that the theatre had to be left spotless and ready for use as soon as possible. Adelaide had just laid the last of the needles away when Night Sister put her head round the door.

'There are relief nurses coming on now; there's breakfast waiting for you as soon as you like.' They smiled at each other, two young women who had done a good night's work, before Night Sister hurried off.

An hour later, breakfasted, shampooed, and very sleepy, Adelaide climbed into bed. She wasn't on until eleven, so she could sleep for an hour or two.

Punctually she walked into the clinic. The waiting room was as full as usual. She went into the office, where the professor, calm and immaculate, sat at his desk. He looked up briefly to answer her good morning, but Piet greeted her with a sigh of relief.

'Thank heaven you're here! I can't find a thing.' He took a second look at her. 'It's a pity the papers can't photograph you now, instead of printing the ones they took of you last night.'

Adelaide, already restoring order among the notes, gazed across at him.

'What do you mean? Did they take some photos? Whatever for?'

'You're in the morning papers; I expect you're in the English papers too.'

She piled some X-rays beside the professor. 'Well, if they're as bad as all that, no one will recognise me,' she said reasonably. She stopped, struck by the thought that her parents, confronted by a photograph of herself taken by flashlight when she was not at her best, might be alarmed. This awful thought was interrupted by a cough from the professor.

'I—er—took the liberty of telephoning your father early this morning. I thought he might be anxious if there should be some mention of the accident in his paper. There probably is, you're a heroine, you know.' His voice was dry.

Adelaide blushed, and for that reason, frowned heavily.

'Thank you very much, sir. It was kind of you to think of it. But what a lot of fuss to make.'

She was fidgeting with a pile of notes, and getting them into a sad state of untidiness. She dropped them like hot coals as the professor said crisply: 'I shall be wanting those in a minute.'

'I'm sorry, sir,' she said meekly, and then, 'Professor?'

He sat back and said encouragingly, 'Yes, Sister?'

She stood in front of him, trying to be composed and cool, and to forget his kiss amidst the ruins of the bus—his fee, he had called it.

'I must thank you for getting me out last night. I was very frightened, you know. It was so dark. I believe you saved our lives, and I am indeed grateful. Just thanking you doesn't seem enough,' she added worriedly.

'Thanking me is quite enough, Sister Peters. It just so happened that I was there. It could have been anyone else, you know.'

She felt surprised at this. 'But I knew it would be you.'

The professor was studying the papers before

him, his pen busy once more, and she didn't expect an answer. She gave a small unconscious sigh.

'Did you and Dr Beekman go to bed? You both look very tired.'

'It was hardly worth it, Sister. We'll go off early if we can.' He glanced up from his work, half smiling. 'Thank you for your solicitude. Now, if you are ready, shall we have the next patient?'

# CHAPTER SIX

THE professor was well known and liked in Amsterdam and the publicity about the bus accident was considerable, but he shrugged it off politely. Adelaide, too, came in for a large share of praise and admiration, which tried and embarrassed her. Miep had been admitted to the ward with fractured ribs and a perforated lung, and she went each day to see her.

A few days after the accident, Miep's parents had found Adelaide in the office. It was not yet nine o'clock, and there was no one else there. They had shaken her by the hand and thanked her over and over again for the part she had played in Miep's rescue. The more they talked, the less she understood, and when at length the professor arrived, she had no hesitation in introducing them to him and slipping out of the room. Ten minutes later she walked quietly into the office again and wished the doctors good morning. Piet Beekman greeted her in his usual friendly way, but the professor, already sitting at his desk, gave her a baleful glance.

'How can you wish me a good morning after the

shabby way you treated me just now? I am surprised at you, Sister. You ran away.'

Adelaide felt indignation swell inside her and began a hot denial, caught the professor's eye and
said rather lamely:

'Well, you didn't need me, sir.'

The professor looked critically at his beautifully
kept nails.

'On the contrary, Sister, I find your presence essential,' he said gently. He looked across at Piet.
'Don't we, Piet?'

Dr Beekman agreed cheerfully. 'Can't find a
thing when you're off duty, Adelaide.'

She laughed. 'What nonsense you talk! You just
don't look.' She turned back to the professor, her
starched apron crackling fiercely.

'Are you ready to start, sir?'

She spoke in a bright, professional voice that
caused both men to look up at her openmouthed;
she had remembered, just in time, her resolve to be
pleasantly friendly but cool, and very, very efficient.

The weather turned warm, the clinic seemed
more crowded than ever. The shops were full of
summer clothes, and holidays were the main topic
of conversation.

Miep was nearly well again, and was going
home in a day or so. Adelaide had bought her a
new dress, ready for the great day, and took it along

to the ward on the evening before Miep was to be discharged. The little girl was sitting up in her bed, playing Snakes and Ladders with the professor, who was lounging on the counterpane, thereby breaking a strict rule enforced by Zuster Zijlstra. He was demanding and accepting advice from the children in the nearby cots, and the noise was considerable. Zuster Zijlstra, writing her report as Adelaide went past her office, shrugged her shoulders and waved her on to the ward. She pushed open the door, took one look, and decided to go back later. Miep hadn't seen her, and the professor's head was bowed over the game. However, she had hardly got her hand on the door handle when he bellowed above the din: 'Don't go away, Sister, I want to see you.'

Adelaide advanced towards the bed. The clinic had finished only an hour ago; she wondered what he could want her for, as he had had plenty of time to speak to her during the day. She hesitated when he patted the counterpane. 'Sit down and don't be a goose. If I can break a rule, so can you.'

He spoke in Dutch, to the great delight of the children, who shouted *'Dag Zuster'* in a deafening manner, and urged her to break the rules like the doctor. Outnumbered, she sat down gingerly on the side of the bed, to be immediately enveloped in Miep's excited embrace. The little girl had seen the dress over Adelaide's arm, and bounced wildly

around the bed, hugging Adelaide until she cried
for mercy.

'The doctor's taking me home,' Miep said im-
portantly. 'In his car.' She beamed at them both.

'Ah, yes.' The professor glanced at Adelaide.
'We thought it would be nice if you came too.
You're off duty tomorrow afternoon, aren't you?
Dr Beekman will take the clinic.'

Adelaide wondered how he knew she was off
duty, and realised that there was nothing to stop
him studying the off-duty rota in her office.

Miep was smiling at her coaxingly. 'You must
come, Adelaide.'

Adelaide smiled back at the child. 'Yes, of
course I'll come.' Her voice was warm and kind.
She turned to the professor. 'What time shall I be
ready, and where shall I meet you, sir?' She was
friendly and pleasant, but her voice was the voice
of a Ward Sister addressing a consultant. Even in
her own ears it sounded prim, and when the professor said quietly: 'You're sure you want to
come?' she cried. 'Oh, yes, please!' with all the
warmth back again, and quite forgetful of the role
she had cast for herself.

The following afternoon she fetched Miep, ra-
diant in her new dress, and went to the clinic entrance. They were very punctual, but the Volvo was
already there. The professor got out and lifted Miep
into the front seat, admired her dress and told her

what a pretty girl she was. She threw her arms around his neck and gave him a smacking kiss. Adelaide, standing and watching, was horrified to hear Miep's voice.

'Now kiss Adelaide and tell her she's got a pretty dress too.'

She saw the professor turn an amused face to her, and took an involuntary step backwards.

'No!' As she said it, she thought how silly she was, when she wanted him to kiss her so much.

'No?' He was laughing at her now 'But I may admire your dress, may I not?'

She thought he was being polite. The dress was plain, pale green and last year's. Her arms were bare, and so were her sandalled feet. She was very conscious of the vividness of her hair in the sunshine and the sprinkling of golden freckles across her nose. She got into the car and he shut the door and leaned over it to ask her if Miep always called her Adelaide.

'Yes, you see I told her that that was my name when we were in the bus.'

When he suggested that he should do the same in order not to confuse the little girl, she agreed readily enough; it seemed a sensible enough suggestion.

It didn't take long to get to Velsen, where Miep lived. They drew up in front of a small terraced house and her whole family came to the door; there seemed to be a great many of them. Everyone went inside, and Adelaide and the professor were escorted into the front parlour, an unlived-in little room, obviously used only on important family occasions. The furniture, by no means modern, had been so polished by zeal and love that it glowed; the small window, shut firmly against dust, was almost obscured by a multitude of pot plants. Even the cushions were plumped up to exact squares.

They all sat around the room, drinking milkless tea and eating a very creamy cake. Adelaide sat between a young man and a big blonde girl; they smiled at her and stared at her hair, but didn't say a word. She looked across at the professor and envied him the steady flow of small talk issuing so effortlessly from his lips. After a little while, he caught her eye, and she stood up and shook hands endlessly, gave Miep a final hug, and got into the car.

'What nice people,' she remarked as he eased the Volvo over the brick road towards the main street, 'and so kind and hospitable. I hoped I would see the rest of the house—they didn't all live in it, did they?'

The professor shook his head. 'No, most of them were cousins and aunts and uncles come to welcome Miep back home. He had halted the car, waiting to join in the continuous stream of traffic on the motorway. Adelaide settled herself firmly into the comfort of well-kept leather. 'What a lovely day—the hottest we've had.'

'You're not on duty until five, are you, Adelaide? There's plenty of time, shall we go to the sea first and perhaps have tea somewhere?'

It was very tempting. Adelaide said 'Yes' before she had stopped to think, and even then she stilled the accusing little thought that she was not keeping to her resolution by the sensible one that she was very unlikely ever to go out with the professor again.

Having absolved her conscience, Adelaide prepared to enjoy her outing. The professor proved to be an excellent companion. She remembered wistfully the evening they had spent together in Amsterdam; he had been a delightful host then, but today he seemed younger and bent on amusing her. By the time they arrived at the Grand Hotel, Huister Duin, she had forgotten all her scruples about his wealth and title, and all her good resolutions, too. They had tea on the terrace, and afterwards, as they had half an hour to spare, strolled along by the water's edge. The breeze whipped her hair around her face, and after a few minutes she took off her sandals and splashed through the water, the professor strolling placidly beside her, smoking his pipe. She didn't talk a great deal, and the professor hardly at all. She paddled along in a happy companionable silence until he looked at his watch.

'We'll have to be going if you don't want to be late on duty, Adelaide.'

They found an upturned boat near the hotel, and she sat down and dried her feet on his handkerchief, put her sandals back on, and then began an ineffectual attempt to tidy her hair, watched lazily by her companion. 'Leave it alone,' he said. 'It looks very nice.' He knocked out his pipe. 'When are you having your holiday?'

Adelaide thrust a last pin into position and said guardedly:

'I don't know.'

'Are you going to England?'

She made a pattern on the sand with her sandal. 'No, I don't think so. I...I thought I'd have a holiday when I get back home.' She made her voice sound cheerful, and looked carefully away out to sea.

'Won't your family be disappointed?' he queried.

She frowned at his persistence, and resisted a strong desire to tell him that she hadn't enough money for the journey, not if she was going to help with the boys' school fees. But of course she couldn't, especially to someone like the professor who, she suspected, never had to think about money anyway. She frowned fiercely at the horizon, and blinked away threatening tears.

His placid voice came from somewhere behind her shoulder.

'A pity you're not taking a couple of weeks during the summer. I'm going over to Dorset at the end of July, and thought you might like a lift there and back. You live somewhere near Rye, don't you? I practically pass your family's doorstep.'

Adelaide didn't answer at once; she had heard what he had said, but she couldn't believe it. She turned her head and said soberly enough:

'You mean I could go home and come back again in your car?' She looked at him searchingly. 'Wouldn't you rather be by yourself?'

'No, I like a travelling companion on a long journey.'

Adelaide bit her lip. A long journey. Just how long? She was, she knew, extremely old-fashioned in many ways, due no doubt to being the daughter of a country parson who still lived according to the standards of his youth. She asked cautiously:

'How long would it take?'

The professor hid his smile very successfully; perhaps because he was a doctor, he was remarkably good at reading other people's thoughts.

'If we leave early, directly after breakfast, you should be home for tea.' He went on, the twinkle in his eye belying the gravity of his tone: 'I took one of the Sisters over with me a couple of years ago—she came to no harm,' he added wickedly.

Adelaide felt her cheeks grow hot. She said with tremendous dignity:

'But I didn't mean—that is, I never...' she looked at him helplessly. 'I'm rather old-fashioned and I don't know how to change.' She was relieved to see him smile again.

'Yes, you are, aren't you? But don't change, Adelaide, we all like you as you are, and there's no need for you to get flustered.' He was mocking her gently again. 'It seems to me it's a sensible idea, and I have always thought you to be a sensible person.'

This remark had the same effect as a bucket of cold water upon Adelaide. She told herself that it was just what she needed to chase away the very silly thoughts that had been floating around her head. It was indeed a very sensible arrangement, made, she reminded herself sternly, between two sensible people. She said politely: 'Thank you very much, Professor, I should be very glad to accept our offer...' He cut her off briskly.

'Good. Get your leave fixed up, then. I should like to go on the nineteenth, that will get us back for early August—plenty of casualties then. Now we'd better go back.'

He said no more about it, but maintained a casual conversation to which Adelaide found herself responding quite cheerfully. He got her to the hospital with five minutes to spare; she wasted one of them standing in the doorway of the Sisters' Home, answering his careless wave, and watching the gleaming car disappear into the maze of narrow streets around the hospital.

She had plenty of time for her thoughts that evening. Casualty had never been so slack—bee stings, wasp stings, sunburn—all could be dealt with without the aid of a doctor. She took as long as possible to clear up and get Casualty ready for the night staff, then walked through to her office where she sat down at her desk and allowed herself to think about her afternoon. Margriet Keizer would probably get to hear about it—Adelaide looked at the clock—the professor was doubtless dining with her somewhere at that very moment. She sighed and opened the day book and started to count the entries. Half way down the page she stopped, struck by the thought that it wouldn't matter in the least if Margriet did know. The professor had neither done nor said anything that even the most jealous of girl-friends could have objected to.

Adelaide lost no time in getting her holiday booked. The very next morning she went to Matron's office and arranged it with the Directrice, who agreed pleasantly that it was indeed too good an opportunity to miss. Besides, she pointed out, it would give Zuster Wilsma a chance to show what she could do. Adelaide hurried back to the clinic, there was still ten minutes before the professor was due to arrive. Should she tell him at once that she could come with him, or wait until their coffee break, or would he mention it first?

The professor didn't come. Piet walked in alone and offered the information that the boss was having a few days off, adding gloomily that it couldn't have been a worse time for him to be away. Adelaide swallowed her disappointment. A few days meant two, three, perhaps four days, so she would have to be patient; in the meantime there was plenty of work to do.

The professor had gone away on the Tuesday, and by Sunday evening there was neither word nor news from him. Adelaide longed to ask, but dared not—Piet was a dear, but a great tease, if she showed any but the most casual interest as to the professor's whereabouts, he would be sure to comment upon it. She held her tongue, worked harder than was needful, and went every evening to the swimming pool outside the city with Zuster Zijlstra and her fiancé and Dr Bos, who had a girl-friend in Giethoorn and talked about her all the time. Adelaide was glad she was on duty that evening. It was hot and close in the clinic and a swim would have been wonderful, but not, she decided, if she had to listen to any more of Henk Bos's tales of his                                         Mia.

She busied herself changing the pillow slips and couch covers and making sure that everything was ready for the morning clinic. Casualty was always full on a Monday; it was as well to have the clinic ready.

She started to fold a pile of towels, wondering for the hundredth time where the professor was. He hadn't taken a holiday since she had arrived at the hospital. He was going to have two weeks in July, that left a month—perhaps he had changed his plans and wasn't going to England after all?

The sing-song wail of the ambulance interrupted her thoughts, and she hurried through to Casualty. It was a small boy, fallen head first from a fourth floor window in a tenement house close to the hospital. She telephoned Dr Beekman, borrowed a nurse from Zuster Zijlstra's ward, and set to work on the child, who was deeply unconscious. He would be an urgent theatre case by the look of things. She sent the nurse to warn Theatre Sister, and waited while Piet examined the boy.

'I've warned the theatre, shall I get Dr Van Hoven?' He nodded. 'We'll have to start at once if he's to have a chance. Any idea when he last had a meal?' He was thinking of the anaesthetic.

She had already asked the child's mother. 'Six o'clock, nothing since, luckily.'

She slid a triangular bandage under the battered little head and tied it loosely under the dressings;

she had already undressed the little boy as far as possible. She watched him being taken to theatre, then started to clear up once more. It was late when she at last reached her room. She had stopped to console the parents as best she could, and then waited to hear the result of the operation—it was a relief to be able to tell them that their small son had a chance to live, slender though it was.

She must have been more tired than she thought, for she overslept. Stopping only for a cup of tea, and catching up a slice of buttered toast in her hand, she dashed over to the clinic, ten minutes late. Casualty was empty, the nurses well ahead with their work in the clinic, she wished them a good morning and went to her office to write up the books and eat her toast. It was already warm, it would be hot later. The day, which had only just begun, seemed to stretch endlessly before her. She flung open the door on a loud sigh. The professor was sitting at her desk, immersed in a pile of notes before him. He looked up, frowning slightly as she banged the door behind her, and said smoothly:

'Good morning, Sister Peters. Forgive me for not getting up; and for appropriating your office—the nurses turned me out of my own room.' He caught sight of the toast, and raised his eyebrows.

Adelaide ignored the eyebrows and said in a formal little voice which effectively concealed her pleasure at seeing him again:

'Good morning, sir. I don't need the office, thank you.' She put the toast down carefully on her desk and picked up the laundry and dispensary books, a box of scalpels for sharpening, and a large bag of mending which the professor had thrown carelessly on the floor. She was at the door when he reminded her gently:

'Don't forget your toast, Adelaide.'

She snatched it up, looking cross, and was half way through the door when he spoke again.

'Will you tell Dr Beekman to come and see me here as soon as he arrives; and you come with him, please.'

Adelaide remembered the casualty of the evening before. Had something gone wrong; had they made some terrible mistake?

'The little boy who was brought in last night—they did a trephine—he's all right, sir?'

He didn't look up. 'In excellent shape, Sister. And now, if you don't mind…'

Adelaide went out, closing the door with an exaggerated care that was far more annoying than the bang she was longing to give. Half an hour later she was back in the office with Piet behind her. This time the professor got up and she sat down in her chair behind the desk, the men one on each side of her. They made the little room seem even smaller. She folded her hands on the starched whiteness of her apron and waited composedly for the professor to speak, her outward serenity covering her true feelings.

'I thought that we would have a picnic,' he began. 'This evening. The clinic staff and Zuster Zijlstra; she'll come, I know. You bring Leen with you, Piet, we'll need your car anyway, I can't get everyone into mine. We'll go to Noordwijk and swim and have supper on the beach.'

Piet grinned. 'A wonderful idea. What do you say, Adelaide?'

She choked back her bitter disappointment. She was on duty that evening and wouldn't be able to go.

'It's a lovely idea,' she said cheerfully.

'Who's the unlucky nurse on duty?' Piet asked.

Adelaide adjusted a cuff to an exact correctness and said ungrammatically: 'Me.' She tried to make her voice sound cheerful. 'Well—er—no, Sister, you're not,' the professor's voice was very smooth. 'I arranged for Zuster Zijlstra's staff nurse to take over at five. That's if you have no objection?'

No, she had no objection. She said so quietly, her heart thumping with happiness, her thoughts racing ahead; arranging the work, contriving how to have the day's work finished on time, regretting the simplicity of her black swim-suit, thankful for the new white bathing cap with that ridiculous fringe. She could press the blue and white striped cotton during the dinner hour... 'Shall we get started, Sister?'

She could tell by the professor's voice that he had already said it once, even twice. She jumped to her feet.

'Of course, sir.' She smiled at him, dazzlingly. 'It's a very heavy clinic too.' Her eyes danced; life, she felt, could be wonderful when you least expected it.

The last little patient left at ten to five, and the entire staff set to with a will to get the clinic tidy. Even the professor stayed behind to help, sitting calmly filing X-rays amidst the ordered chaos of clearing up. Adelaide eyed him lovingly; she thought he looked tired and rather sad. She wondered if Margriet had refused to marry him after all, and her heart leapt at the thought. He lifted his head, and she looked away quickly, ashamed to feel so happy for such a reason.

Zuster Zijlstra was almost ready when Adelaide got to her room.

'Hallo, Adelaide. Hurry!'

Adelaide needed no second bidding. She tore off her uniform, showered and dressed, and then stuffed the despised black swim-suit into her beach bag, she added the new swim-cap and a short towelling coat, gathered up her bag, and pronounced herself ready.

They were the last to arrive. Zuster Wilsma was

in Piet's car. Zuster Eisink and Zuster Steensma were sharing the back of the Volvo with the professor's two dogs. He was waiting with the car door open.

'Adelaide, Leen wants to gossip; you'd better go with Piet.'

She slipped obediently into the seat beside Leen, and listened smilingly to Leen's account of little Piet's amazing cleverness without hearing a word of it.

They went through Noordwijk and past the main beach, until the professor finally stopped at a small secluded arc of sand, empty but for a couple of gaily striped tents, and a handful of the wickerwork hooded chairs so beloved by the Dutch and so coveted by the British. They came to life as the cars stopped. Adelaide recognised the professor's sisters and their children; she supposed the two men with them were their husbands. They were all enveloped in a happy laughing mass and hurried off to change and thence to the water's edge where a ball game was in progress.

She looked around for the professor and saw him in the water, on his back and supporting a small boy on each arm. The little boys were shouting and laughing; the professor appeared to be asleep. The ball game became hectic, with a great deal of splashing and short sharp bursts of swimming. Adelaide, racing to retrieve the ball, saw the diving board moored some distance out from the shore. She was a strong swimmer; it looked very tempting. She didn't think she would be missed if she swam quickly there, had a couple of dives, and then back. She ducked away, and when she was clear of the others, changed to the crawl, tunnelling through the clear water, head well down; so it was that she missed the professor as he passed her, going very fast and quietly. He was waiting for her when she reached the board and heaved her up with a powerfully muscled arm.

They sat side by side, getting their breath and dangling their feet in the water. The sun was still warm on their bodies. Adelaide was trying to think of something to say—she longed to know if the trip to England had been arranged, but perhaps it would sound a little too eager if she asked him. Instead she said:

'What a beautiful evening.'

'Very.'

She tried again:

'And such a beautiful beach.'

'Very beautiful.'

She went bravely on. 'The water's warm too.'

'Yes.'

She was suddenly exasperated. 'Don't you want to talk?'

She quite forgot to say 'sir'.

'Yes, I do, when you've finished discussing the landscape.'

Adelaide went pink. 'I'm making conversation; it's polite,' she snapped. She watched him laughing and almost choked on a childish rage which melted completely at his next words.

'You know about my eye, don't you?'

She turned and looked at him deliberately and said softly:

'Yes, I do. I'm sorry.'

He continued placidly. 'I've been in Vienna; there's a good man there. Sometimes I get impatient—wanting a miracle, I suppose. The only one he gave me was a pair of new glasses.'

Adelaide tried to keep her voice normal. 'And has it helped?'

'Oh, yes,' he said cheerfully. 'The small grey blurs are now large grey blurs.'

She marvelled at the lack of bitterness in his voice.

'How did you find out that I knew?' Surely Mijnheer de Wit hadn't told him, or had she, shameful thought, made herself conspicuous by looking at him too often? She had to know.

'You always stand on my good side when we're at work.' He changed the conversation abruptly. 'I've got the trip to England arranged.'

She gave a sigh of relief. 'I thought that perhaps you had changed your plans, and we weren't going.' She frowned. 'How did you know that I had arranged my holiday for the last two weeks in July?'

'I rang the Directrice.'

There was a great commotion behind them, at least half the picnic party were about to board them. Adelaide felt a large hand between her shoulders. 'In you go,' said the professor, and gave her a push.

They all spent some time diving and swimming around the board, and when they were tired out, swam in a body back to the beach, where the lazier members of the party had set the picnic ready.

Adelaide surveyed the food spread out on the gay cloths with something approaching awe. Lobster patties, golden brown chicken legs, with elegant pink frills, vol-au-vents spilling something delectable over golden pastry, baby sausage rolls, minute pork pies, cheese of every sort, baskets of fruit. It seemed to her unsophisticated eye more like a banquet without its usual background than a picnic on the beach. She sat between a quiet youngish man, whom she identified as a brother-in-law of the professor, and a boy of about ten, who addressed the quiet man as Uncle. They plied her with food, and flattered her subtly by carrying on a conversation in Dutch, helping her unobtrusively when she stumbled over a word. It was, she thought, the

nicest picnic she had ever been to. She turned to
her companion and asked:

'Do you live here?' She looked round; there was
no house to be seen on the dunes.

He waved vaguely inland. 'We have a summer
villa; we spend as much time here as we can in the
summer. The whole family come—Coenraad is
here most weekends. You should come too,
Adelaide,' he added kindly.

'You're very kind, but I'm not often off duty at
the weekends.' Too late she realized that she had
taken it for granted that she would be invited with
the professor, and her cheeks flamed. If her companion noticed he made no comment, but said
merely:

'A pity, but you must come when you can.'

'Thank you, Mijnheer Tesselaar de Klerk.' She
was pleased that she had remembered his name.

'And for heaven's sake call me Cor!'

It was cooler now; the girls had put on their
beach coats and the men wore an assortment of
sweaters and shirts. They looked like a band of
gipsies. Only the smallest of the children were still
tearing around in the briefest of garments. They
drank the last of the fragrant coffee and started to
pack up the remains of the feast. It was a leisurely
task, interlarded with a considerable amount of
talk; by the time they were ready, it was a deep
twilight.

They wandered back to the cars and said protracted good nights while children were caught and stowed away, protesting sleepily. Adelaide started towards Piet's car, but was stopped by a hand on her shoulder. 'Over here, Adelaide.' The professor opened the door of the Volvo; Zuster Steensma and Zuster Eisink were already in the back, the dogs sitting damply at their feet.

'In you get.' She got in, and watched him go round to the other side and slide into the seat beside her. He was wearing a baggy old sweater over his slacks, which made him seem very large in the dim light. He backed the car, and they went back the way they had come, through the quiet evening. The journey to the hospital seemed very short; afterwards she couldn't remember a word of what had been said, only that she had thanked him before they had all got out of the car, and he had cut her short by saying:

'Please don't thank me—it is I who should thank my excellent nursing staff for their unceasing hard work.'

He had said it very pleasantly, but that hadn't prevented her from feeling that now that the picnic was over, she had been put firmly back in her place.

# CHAPTER SEVEN

IT was a glorious morning when the Rolls slid away from the hospital. It was still early, but the clinic staff were all there to give Adelaide and the professor a rousing send-off. Adelaide's case had been put in the boot, and the nurses had gathered round her, wishing her a happy holiday rather wistfully. She cheered them up with the news that she would be sure to bring back something for each of them, and got into the car, settled in her seat, and opened the road map the professor had thoughtfully provided for her. They were going via Utrecht and Breda and Bruges and then to Calais, because she didn't know that part of Holland; and although they wouldn't have much time to stop, it would be interesting to see another part of the charming little country.

They turned into the Churchilllaan, and were immediately hailed from the pavement by Margriet Keizer. Coenraad brought the car to a halt, and they sat waiting for her to reach them. She looked cool and crisp and beautifully turned out in a white dress which Adelaide guessed was couture. She put a hand fleetingly on the professor's, as it rested on the wheel, and smilingly greeted them both. Adelaide noticed with satisfaction that the professor gently removed the hand and put his own on his knee.

'Surely this is early for you to be out, Margriet?'

She ignored the edge of sarcasm in his voice. 'Yes, I know, but I have some shopping to do.' She glanced at Adelaide, eyeing her pale blue dress with thinly veiled contempt.

'How fortunate for you, Miss Peters, that Baron Van Essen is going to England, and you had the chance of a lift.' Her mouth curved in a smile that didn't quite reach her lovely eyes. 'I do so admire you nurses, working for a pittance—barely enough to dress on, I should imagine.'

Adelaide was determined to keep her temper, and stated fairly:

'Well, we wear uniform for most of the day, so we don't need many clothes.'

Margriet's eyes flickered over the blue dress. 'Yes, I expect you're able to make your things last for years.'

Adelaide remembered, just in time, that she was a clergyman's daughter. 'Yes, I do,' she replied quite gently. Margriet turned back to Coenraad.

'Why didn't you let me know that you had planned a trip to England? I suppose you thought that I was booked up for the summer. We could have had a wonderful time.' She shot a quick look at Adelaide, sitting so quietly. 'The Baron and I have known each other all our lives.' Her voice was honeyed.

'I've known that for a long time,' Adelaide replied, and before she could say more, the professor said curtly:

'I had always thought that you disliked England?'

Margriet looked put out, and then laughed.

'That's true, but I suppose that I could even like England if I were with you, Coenraad.'

Adelaide was looking steadily ahead of her, apparently engrossed in the passing traffic. She had no intention of allowing Margriet the small triumph of knowing that she had upset her. She went on watching the street in an unruffled calm until Margriet, finding the professor unresponsive, at last made her farewells and, with a final wave, left them. The professor started up the car once more without speaking, and Adelaide busied herself with her map. It was quite two minutes before he broke the silence.

'I must admire your forbearance, Miss Peters. Margriet is sometimes rather tactless, but I imagine that you are far too sensible a young woman to let anything she said annoy you.'

Adelaide closed the map with an unnecessary violence, her brown eyes flashing. To be addressed as a sensible young woman so soon after Margriet's thinly veiled sneers was really too much for her good nature. She sat upright, her hands gripping her handbag as though it were Margriet's throat. She spoke deliberately, between her teeth.

'Pray don't trouble yourself about my feelings, Professor—or should I say Baron?' Despite herself her voice shook a little. She kept her eyes on the road ahead of her, not caring if he answered her or not. They were travelling very fast; the professor seemed bent on overtaking everything in sight. She stole a quick peep at him. He was laughing. He said in gently mocking tones:

'You are in a bad temper, aren't you?' His voice changed, she had never heard it quite so harsh. 'And you are not to call me Baron, now, or at any other time.'

She said stubbornly, 'Why not?'

'Because neither my family nor my friends address me as such.'

She was in a mood to argue. 'You forget, Professor, that I am a nurse, working for you.'

'No, I haven't forgotten,' he smiled briefly, 'but I count you among my friends, you know, and since we are friends I shall call you Adelaide until we get back to work, and then I promise that you shall be Miss Peters again. Could you not call me Coenraad, on the strict understanding, of course, that I become a professor again the moment I walk into the clinic?'

She had to laugh at this. 'Yes, I should like that, and I'm sorry I was cross just now.' Her good temper was quite restored. She was, after all, on holiday. Margriet seemed very far away, and she had the whole day to look forward to. She opened the map again and started picking out their route. The breeze was blowing her hair gently on her down-bent head, she put up a hand and brushed a loose strand away from her forehead, with the unself-conscious gesture of a child. She was absorbed in her map reading, and quite unaware of the charming picture she made.

They drove steadily south; the car needed little urging. Adelaide sat quietly, watching Coenraad. She liked the way he drove, with a minimum of movement and fuss. As they approached Breda, they were held up for a few minutes in a small village, where the local band, banners flying, was proceeding down the main street. They were playing *Piet Hein*, and Coenraad took up the refrain, whistling under his breath. Adelaide, who recognised the tune and had been taught to whistle by her brothers, joined in, and they whistled their way through a selection of tunes for the remainder of the road to the border, where the *douane* waved them by with a cheerful salute.

Adelaide abandoned her whistling for questions about the countryside through which they were passing, which the professor patiently answered.

She was disappointed in Belgium; it looked untidy and faintly neglected after the neat houses and gardens of Holland.

It was a pity that there was no time to stop at Bruges; it looked delightful, but the professor drove straight through the town without pause. He had had to slow down because of the stretches of cobbled street, it was a relief when they were once more on the main road. They swept through Ostend, and presently, Veurne. It seemed the *douane* here was just as uninterested in them as the first one had been. Adelaide looked around her.

'I've been in three countries in one morning,' she said naïvely.

'Four by tea-time,' he reminded her.

That put her in mind of something, and she said rather shyly:

'Mother would like it if you would stay to tea with us.' She paused. 'That is, unless you have other plans?'

'None,' he replied cheerfully, 'and if you hadn't asked me, I daresay I should have invited myself. I hope you're hungry now, I thought we would have a meal before we go on board.'

They made their way through Calais down to the docks, and watched while the car was loaded aboard, then walked back to the town, where he took her to a small restaurant in a side street. It had red check tablecloths on the few tables scattered on the scrubbed floor; it surprised her to see that the people sitting at them were very smart. Adelaide had no idea that it was famous for its cuisine. She looked at the menu card and put it down again.

'I don't know anything about French food, so please will you choose for me?'

When it came, the food was delicious, and she paid him the compliment of eating a hearty meal and listening intelligently to his comments upon French cooking.

Afterwards, when Adelaide tried to remember the crossing on the boat, she found it difficult to recall any clear memories of it. She only knew that the professor had been a delightful companion, and that the time had flown so fast that she was amazed to see the cliffs of Dover looming up out of the summer haze.

It was just tea-time when they turned into the short curving drive of the rectory. Adelaide looked round happily. The rectory was a small Regency house, with a square porch and large windows on either side. It was shabby as to paint, but the garden was well tended and a riot of colour. She looked at Coenraad, who said before she could speak: 'It's delightful; I can't think of a better place in which to have tea.'

At that moment one of the windows opened and a grey-haired gentleman looked out. He waved and withdrew, to reappear a moment later at the front door, in time to engulf Adelaide, who had jumped out of the car, in a fatherly hug. She had time to introduce Coenraad before her mother came running out of the house. She was very like her daughter, with the same very red hair, beginning to fade a little, but still an arresting colour. She kissed her daughter and shook the professor warmly by the hand before summoning Adelaide's brothers, clamouring around their sister. They were sixteen years old, and identical twins, big for their age, with fair hair and their father's mild blue eyes. They said 'how do you do' with proper respect, but within a very few minutes were involved in an animated discussion concerning the hidden beauties of the Rolls-Royce engine. The Reverend Mr Peters brought this to an end, however, by telling the boys to let Nellie know that Adelaide had arrived. The two gentlemen then repaired indoors to join the family for tea. As they crossed the hall, a short, stout, elderly woman came through the baize door under the stairs, and stopped when she saw them.

'Tea's ready, Reverend.' She spoke to her master, but looked at the professor, her sharp old eyes raking him from his dark well-brushed hair to his exquisitely polished shoes. He bore her scrutiny with good nature, and when she was introduced as the mainstay and friend of the entire family, remarked that they were indeed fortunate to have her. The two men watched as Adelaide came through

the door and flung her arms round Nellie's neck,
to be greeted with a 'There, Miss Addy, it'll be
nice to have you home for a bit, and now go and
eat your tea, there's a nice wholesome cake I made.
It'll do you good after all that foreign food.'

Tea was a gay meal, with a great deal of laughter
and chatter. Adelaide, sitting by her mother, was
able to watch the professor where he sat, discussing
the works of Bacon with Mr. Peters. Listening to
snatches of their talk, she decided that the professor
must be a very clever man to earn her father's ap-
probation on a subject in which he was considered
something of an expert. They had eaten all the
sandwiches and had cut deep into Nellie's cake,
when her mother said, 'I'm going to talk to that
nice professor, Addy dear, and send your father to
talk to you.'

Mr Peters, his serious talk curtailed firmly by his
wife, wandered over to sit by his daughter, to question her about her life in Holland. Adelaide answered willingly enough, but as she was listening
to her mother's conversation as well as she was
able, she was somewhat distraite, a fact which her
father put down to her long journey. Her mother
had a quiet voice; Adelaide found that she was unable to hear a word. To look at the professor's face
was of no use. It bore his usual placid expression.
He wasn't saying much, but he smiled, and once
looked across the room directly at her in a thought-

ful way. She wondered what they were talking about.

They were talking about her; her mother had thanked Coenraad for bringing Addy home. 'We've been longing to see her.' She turned a little pink, and said with the same engaging candour as her daughter, 'She wanted to come home so badly, but the boys are to stay another year at school and she helps.' She raised her brown eyes, so like Addy's, to her companion, who said nothing, but was listening with interest. 'They're very clever, and deserve their chance. In a year or two we shall be able to paint the house and have a new car, and Addy can spend all her money on herself, bless her.' She looked fondly at her daughter.

Adelaide saw the faint, amused smile on the professor's face and wondered what her mother had been saying. She would have liked to have joined them, but her mother was deep in conversation again.

'We've been waiting to thank you for going to Addy's rescue in that bus; she didn't say much about it, although we read about it in the papers. She told us that she owed her escape and perhaps her life to you. We are indeed most grateful to you, Professor.'

He looked embarrassed. 'There were a dozen men waiting to do what I did,' he replied. 'I just happened to be the nearest. Adelaide was the brave

one.' He told Mrs. Peters what had happened at
some length.

Adelaide, from the other side of the room, wondered what they could be talking about so ear-
nestly. She went over to the tea tray to refill her
father's cup, and lingered long enough to hear her
mother invite the professor to stay the night, and
his regretful refusal. He had, he said, promised to
arrive at his destination by ten o'clock that evening.
Adelaide gave her father his cup and went and sat
by her mother, just in time to hear Coenraad say,
in answer to her mother's question:

'Yes, a very old friend. I couldn't disappoint her,
she is someone of whom I am very fond.' He didn't
add that the old friend was his childhood's nanny,
installed as his housekeeper in the small manor
house which his English grandmother had left him.

'Then stay on your way back,' said Mrs Peters
and Adelaide felt a little thrill of delight when he
said yes, he would like that very much. He got up
to go shortly afterwards, and made his goodbyes.

Adelaide stood by her father, listening to Coenraad's quiet voice, and realised that she wouldn't
hear it again for two weeks. She gave him her hand
and thanked him for her lovely day and wished him
a pleasant holiday in a subdued voice. His hand felt
oddly comforting as she put her own into it. When
she looked up into his face she saw that his eyes
were dancing with laughter, and thought uneasily

that he might be reading her thoughts. She was glad when her mother spoke.

'Why not come to lunch, Professor Van Essen? Nellie will cook you a lovely wholesome English meal, and Addy shall make an apple pie.'

He accepted with alacrity, and released Adelaide's hand without speaking again to her. She stood waving with the others as he drove away without looking at her.

The professor arrived at the rectory about midday, at least an hour earlier than he had said. As he got out of the car at the open front door, Matthew and Mark came dashing out to meet him. They were delighted to see him again, though he suspected that their interest might be more for his car than himself. Mr Peters put his head out of his study window and begged him to come in at once and not to allow the boys to bother him. They all went indoors together and into the study, where Mrs Peters sat knitting and keeping her husband company. They all talked at once, and he thought what a happy family they were. When he apologised for being early, Mrs Peters said cheerfully, 'But we've all been waiting for you to arrive. Addy's in the kitchen, why not go and tell her you're here, for I'm sure she must be finished by now.'

Adelaide stood at the kitchen table, rolling pastry, and taking her time about it. Coenraad wasn't due for another hour, it stretched ahead of her endlessly, but if she was busy the time might go a little faster. The door opened behind her. It would be her mother, come to see if she was ready.

'He might not like apple pie,' she said.

'He loves it.' She was quite unprepared for his voice, and spun round to face him, her heart beating a tattoo against her ribs to shake her. She quelled her desire to fling her floury arms around his neck and tell how glad she was to see him, and instead frowned darkly.

'You're early,' she said. 'Look at me.' And was vexed when, without further words, he did so. She stood in front of him, in a cotton dress almost covered by a large apron, her hair tied back in an untidy pony-tail. She remembered that she hadn't any make-up on. She felt her cheeks grow hot under his gaze, and with a forlorn little gesture turned back to the table and bent over her pastry. She didn't look up when he came and sat on the edge of the table.

'You told me to look at you,' he said reasonably, and ate some pastry. 'I'm sorry I'm early. Shall I go away and come back again when you've had time to put up your hair and turn into the cool and composed Miss Peters?'

Despite herself, Adelaide burst out laughing.

'That's better,' he said. 'I was beginning to think you weren't glad to see me.' He absent-mindedly ate some more pastry. 'You look very nice as you are, Addy.'

She drew the pie dish towards her and gently laid her dough over the apples therein. She didn't look at him, because he would be laughing at her, and she didn't think she could bear that. She was making an edge to her pie, her eyes intent, the black lashes curling on her cheeks.

'Have you had a good holiday, Addy?'

Adelaide raised her brown eyes to his, her smile very sweet; she had quite forgotten her appearance.

'I've had a lovely time!'—her face glowed—'I'll never be able to thank you for letting me come with you. Did you have a good time too?'

'Oh, yes,' said the professor. He sounded rather non-committal. 'I don't suppose it was as much fun as yours.'

She considered this. 'Well, the boys were home.' She smiled warmly at him. She was so happy she wanted to smile all the time. She pushed a long strand of hair out of her eyes, leaving a trail of flour down one cheek. He leaned forward and wiped it away with his handkerchief, then kissed the cheek. Adelaide gasped and turned her head. His face was very close, his eyes full of laughter. Her breath caught in her throat and she seemed, regrettably, to have lost all control over her breathing.

The kitchen door opened and they drew apart as Nellie, laden with washing from the garden, came in. She tossed it into the big basket by the window and came over to the table, and said in scolding tones: 'Now, Miss Addy, that pie'll never get baked if you don't put it in the oven this instant.'

Adelaide picked up the pie obediently, glad of something to do, took it over to the Aga and spent an unnecessarily long time arranging it in the oven, while her cheeks cooled.

Nellie turned her attention to the professor. 'Good morning, sir, and it's nice to see you again. You've had a fine holiday, I'll be bound. The girls all over you and never a dull moment!'

Adelaide banged the oven door, whirled round, and said in a choking voice: 'Nellie!'

'Well, Miss Addy dear, I'm not meaning to be disrespectful, but the professor's a handsome man—you'll allow that, surely? A real nice gentleman, I call him. Why, you said so yourself!'

Adelaide felt her just cooled cheeks redden once more, and she didn't look at the professor when she spoke.

'You're a flatterer, Nellie. You can't expect Miss Addy to agree with you, she works with me every day and sees only my worst side.'

Adelaide caught his brief glance as she stood at the table, cleaning up. She felt goaded.

'I'm usually far too busy to waste time on your looks or your character, Professor.' She spoke tartly, hating herself for the cheap remark. Her words shocked Nellie, but he only laughed, and laughed again when Nellie said, 'Hoity-toity, Miss Addy, that's no answer.'

Coenraad grinned wickedly. 'She's right, you know, Nellie. I mustn't work her so hard, then she will have more time to study me.'

He cocked an eyebrow at Adelaide, who started to laugh—indeed, she felt that if she did not laugh she would burst into tears. She went meekly over to the sink when Nellie said:

'Miss Addy, you go and wash your hands and face and put up that hair this minute! What the professor thinks of you I do not know.'

Adelaide supposed it must be amusing for him to see how obediently his efficient clinic Sister obeyed this order. She took off her apron and was washing her hands when he strolled over and stood beside her. 'Nellie wants to know what I think of you, Addy. Don't you want to know, too?'

She didn't dare look up from drying her hands, but shook her head, flung the towel down and ran across the kitchen without looking at him at all and through the door, banging it hard behind her.

As she came into the study twenty minutes later, her father was pouring the sherry. In that time she had contrived to turn herself into a cool and poised young lady, freshly lipsticked, and not a hair out of place. She stood in the doorway and was glad when the professor saw her and came over and handed her a glass.

He looked her over coolly. 'An excellent imitation of Miss Peters, if I may say so, Adelaide.'

She smiled uncertainly, feeling shy, and not quite sure what to say. She was saved from replying by the arrival of Matthew, who looked at her in astonishment and asked:

'Good heavens, Addy, you're not going out, are you? You've put your hair up too.'

She ignored his brotherly candour with icy composure, taking care not to meet Coenraad's gaze, and listened to her companions discussing the little jaunt they had planned for the afternoon. Down the Brighton road was an enjoyable prospect for a sixteen-year-old boy. She envied her brothers with all her heart.

Adelaide spent the afternoon packing. She had been rather silent during luncheon. Her father had remarked upon it, and her mother had looked across the table, smiled at her and said:

'Addy's a little sad because her holiday is almost over, aren't you, darling?' and Adelaide had smiled back and said 'Yes,' and had done her best to believe it herself. However, when she came downstairs at tea-time, she seemed in the best of spirits and greeted the returned motorists with every sign of good humour. The professor had brought a large box of chocolates for Mrs Peters, and sat beside her during tea, listening to her gentle conversation, and afterwards helped carry the tea things back to the kitchen. It was explained to him that Nellie always put her feet up in the afternoons. The boys were left to wash up, and the others strolled back to the drawing room where Adelaide remarked that she should go and finish her packing, and as nobody suggested that she should do otherwise, she presently went upstairs, where she stood at her bedroom window watching her parents, with Coenraad between them, walking off in the direction of the church. They appeared to be enjoying their conversation, and had apparently forgotten all about her.

Supper was a simple meal. When it was over, they clustered around the table in the study and played Monopoly—a game Mr Peters was much addicted to. Being a poor man, the mythical thousands he lost and won afforded him great pleasure. At ten o'clock, however, his wife said firmly that they would not play any more.

'These two have to leave early in the morning, and they have a long journey before them.'

She set off to the kitchen, leaving Adelaide to tidy away the game. The boys had gone to bed, her father and Coenraad were discussing Greek mythology. She looked out of the open window; the garden, patterned in bright moonlight, was beautiful. She put the cards away in a drawer in her father's desk. Both men seemed engrossed in their conversation; that Reverend Mr Peters, happy to have found someone who could quote Greek poetry in the original, certainly had no eyes for the moonlight. Neither, apparently, had the professor. She emptied an ashtray with unnecessary noise, sighed soundlessly, and went to kiss the bald patch on her father's head. She said good night to the top button of Coenraad's waistcoat, and went upstairs to bed.

The morning was glorious. As Adelaide got into the car she thought that the garden had never looked so lovely. She hated saying goodbye; she waved until the little group standing at the Rectory gate was hidden by the curve of the road, and then sat back very quiet. The tears she had been holding back spilled over and ran slowly down her cheeks, and when a large white handkerchief was proffered wordlessly by the professor, she accepted it with a grateful sniff, mopped her eyes, blew her nose in a no-nonsense fashion, and said in a watery voice:

'Thank you. I didn't mean to cry. Father says that a snivelling female is one of the most tiresome afflictions man is called upon to endure.'

He laughed. 'I admire your father. We had a most interesting talk last night.'

'What about?'

'Oh, metaphysics. He was able to tell me a great

deal about ontology.' He paused. 'He gave me some excellent advice about other matters, too.'

At the thought of her father, she swallowed another hard lump of tears, and said, determinedly cheerfully:

'That's funny. Father never gives advice unless he's certain that it will be taken.' She wondered what Coenraad could possibly want advice about, but he wasn't going to tell her, saying merely:

'But I have every intention of taking it,' and then changing the conversation so pointedly that she knew she must ask no more questions.

She powdered her small red nose and applied herself to the task of being an agreeable companion. This entailed listening intelligently to the professor's views on coarse fishing, of which she knew nothing. She had the good sense not to ask why it was coarse in the first place, she had in fact only a very sketchy knowledge of the sport, but it was pleasant listening to the professor talking, and thus pleasurably occupied, the journey to the car ferry seemed surprisingly short, and even the long wait in the queue to go aboard went unnoticed.

Once aboard, they walked briskly round the deck until the cliffs of Dover were sufficiently far away for her to be able to look at them without feeling homesick, and it wasn't until later that she realised Coenraad's thoughtfulness in engineering their perambulations. By the time they had a cup of coffee, they were docking at Calais, and the slow process of disembarking began. Coenraad had said nothing about lunch. Adelaide wondered about it as they at last emerged from the Customs shed and made slow progress through the town. Now he left the main road and after threading through several narrow streets, stopped outside the restaurant they had visited previously. Obedient to his injunction to remain where she was, she waited quietly until he returned, followed by a waiter carrying a hamper which was stowed carefully in the boot. The professor got back into the car and nursed it carefully over the atrocious cobbles until they joined the N40.

'I thought we'd have a picnic. We'll stop the other side of Ostend, there's a golf course there between the main road and the sea. We'll have lunch there and go over the border at Sluis.'

Adelaide, who would have cheerfully eaten yesterday's bread and a heel of cheese, so long as it was in Coenraad's company, thought this an excellent idea. They bowled along, with only the shortest delay at the French border. An hour later they were going through Ostend. They left the car by the side of the road and scrambled over the dunes until they could see the sea from the shelter of some trees.

Adelaide, unpacking the hamper, thought that the contents, though not as numerous as the dishes served at the clinic picnic, looked just as delicious. She arranged the paper cloth thoughtfully provided and laid the chicken mousse, green salad, thin bread and butter and fruit carefully upon it. She surveyed the result of her work, and said, 'This isn't a picnic. A picnic is sandwiches and thermos flasks. This is a feast!'

Coenraad opened the bottle he had carefully removed before she examined the basket. He filled the glasses and handed her one, and said '*Proost.*' She took a cautious sip, while he watched her smilingly. 'It's quite harmless, Addy.'

Adelaide felt herself grow pink, took a defiant gulp and choked. He had to thump her back while she whooped trying to get her breath. He was nice about it, and didn't laugh until she had enough breath to laugh with him. They ate everything, while she listened to preposterous tales of his student days, only half believing them. When the last crumb had disappeared, she packed everything tidily back in the hamper, while he sat back against a tree, smoking. She was startled when he asked:

'Do you go out much in Amsterdam, Adelaide?'

She sat back on her heels and considered his question.

'No, not a great deal. Once or twice with Dr Bos…'

The professor blew a smoke ring, and remarked quietly:

'He'll miss you while you're away.'

'Good gracious, no. He's gone to Giethoorn; there aren't any roads there,' she explained, airing her knowledge. 'His girl-friend lives there. He told me all about her; no one else wants to listen, you see.'

Coenraad digested this interesting piece of information, and rolled over on to an elbow. 'Who else have you been out with?'

'Well, I went to Haarlem to an organ recital. I enjoyed it, it was a wonderful church too…' she hesitated. 'I went with Dr Vos. He's in the Path Lab,' she added unnecessarily, and felt indignant when the professor laughed.

'Addy! He must be sixty—and a widower.'

'I know, that's why I went.' She saw his raised eyebrows, and hurried on to explain. 'I mean he's almost old, isn't he? I didn't know he was going to…well…' She stopped. 'He was horrid!'

Coenraad sat up leisurely, and asked with interest: 'What did he do?'

She studied her hands. 'He was—unpleasant, and I got annoyed.' She spoke with hauteur, her cheeks pink with temper, her eyes flashing, her beguiling little bosom heaving like a temperamental film star's, just at the remembrance of it. She had for the moment forgotten the professor, who had his eyes closed. She went on:

'Of course, I go to Leen's flat quite often, and I go out with Zuster Zijlstra and Zuster Boot too.'

They fell to discussing the delights of Amsterdam until Coenraad, seeing the time said that they must be off. He helped her to her feet, and they went back to the car.

They reached the outskirts of Amsterdam just before seven o'clock. They had stopped in Delft for tea, and wandered around the charming little town, the professor obligingly bearing her uncomplaining company while she inspected a variety of shops. Now he slowed the Rolls down to weave his way through the evening traffic. Adelaide had become rather quiet. Tomorrow would be reality again, and she tried not to think of it. Her gloomy thoughts were interrupted by Coenraad's voice. 'There's a letter in the pocket next to you, Addy. Will you take it out and read it?'

She did as he had asked. 'It's in Dutch,' she said.

'Yes, read it out loud, it will be excellent practice for you.'

She obeyed, reading in her careful Dutch. When she had come to the end, he said: 'I must compliment you on your progress, Adelaide,' and she felt a thrill of pride. She must remember to tell Mijnheer de Wit. She waited for Coenraad to speak, and when he didn't, said:

'How kind of the Baroness, but I think I had

better go straight back to the hospital, if you don't mind.'

'I do mind—and my aunt will be very disappointed.'

Adelaide frowned. 'I'm not dressed,' she said stubbornly.

'Nor am I. Besides, you can tidy your hair and all the rest of it at Tante Anneke's.'

She could think of no argument in the fact of his reasonable tones, and he swung the car into the Herengracht and drew up before his aunt's house. The big house door was flung open by a beaming Bundle, who surely had been lying in wait for them. He led them to the small parlour where the Baroness liked to sit. She was there now, erect in her chair, beautifully dressed, and obviously delighted to see them both. She put up her cheek for Coenraad to kiss and took Adelaide's hand.

'You nice child, to take pity on my curiosity. I want to hear all about England. Ring the bell, Coenraad. Jannie can show Adelaide where she can freshen up.'

Adelaide went downstairs some ten minutes later to find Coenraad waiting for her. As they crossed the hall, he said easily:

'I've been telling Tante Anneke about your clever brothers.'

This was a subject near to her heart, and she was drawn so skilfully into the conversation that by the time they were half way through dinner she had lost her shyness, and was enjoying herself. Nevertheless, when she presently got up to go to the hospital, and was pressed by her hostess to visit her again soon, she accepted with a hidden reluctance.

Only the preceding night, lying in bed listening to the murmur of her father's and the professor's voices, she had resolved to see as little as possible of him once they were back in Holland, and she knew that he was a frequent visitor to his aunt's house. It had seemed simple to make the decision then; now she was not so sure. She had not forgotten Margriet.

They didn't speak on the short journey to the hospital. Coenraad got her case out of the boot and gave it to a night porter to take over to the home, then walked across the courtyard with her. He opened the door, but when she went to pass through she found her way barred by the careless hand he was resting against it. She stood still.

'Remind me to call you Miss Peters tomorrow.'

She laughed. 'You won't forget. I'll be in uniform, you know.'

'The clinics will be packed out. They always are after the summer holiday.'

They stood silently. Adelaide knew that she must make an end to her fairy tale. She gave him her hand. 'It was lovely—today, I mean. Thank you, and thank you for taking me in your car. It's like waking up from a beautiful dream. Good night…Coenraad.'

She slipped through the door.

# CHAPTER EIGHT

THE professor had been right; the clinics had never been so busy, and they were booked to capacity for two or three weeks ahead. Adelaide looked through the appointments book the next morning and hoped that Casualty would be slack, though there wasn't much chance of that. Indeed, just before nine o'clock, a woman rushed in with an unconscious child in her arms. Adelaide made out with some difficulty that the little boy had swallowed some pills a short time earlier. She sent the nurse to phone Dr Beekman and set about treatment. She had got the airway in, and succeeded in getting the stomach tube down, when she heard footsteps. She recognised them at once, and spoke without stopping her work. 'Good morning, sir. An overdose— unknown pills taken between seven o'clock and now. Unconscious for about ten minutes, his mother says.' She indicated the woman standing in the doorway with her free hand. She started to syphon carefully, and didn't turn around.

'Keep that up, Sister, I'll see to the injections.' He was already opening the phials and drawing up the contents. He questioned the mother quietly as he pushed in the needle, working quickly and smoothly. Adelaide, still busily syphoning, thought what a nice person he was to work with in an emergency. She couldn't remember seeing him hesitant or anxious, she had never seen him really angry either. She doubted if she ever would.

They worked on the child in a partnership of shared knowledge and skill, not speaking until presently the professor said:

'He'll do.' He turned away and asked Piet, who had just come in, if there were any beds. Piet nodded. The professor walked to the door.

'Good, let's have him in for a day or two. I'll talk to the mother.' He turned to go, saying over his shoulder: 'Out-Patients in ten minutes, Sister.'

Adelaide looked at the mess around her, and Piet laughed at her expressive face.

'I'll take the child to the ward, it'll give you more time to clear up.'

Adelaide sent the nurse along to warn Staff Wilsma to be ready for the professor, she herself would have to stop and show the nurse, sent to replace Zuster Eisink who was on holiday, and new to the work, what to clear up and what to get ready. It took longer than she had thought it would, and the clinic was well started as she went down the corridor. She could hear the professor's voice as she opened the door; it was quiet but had a distinct edge to it. She found him sitting with his head mirror on, waiting to examine the small boy Zuster Wilsma was vainly trying to hold on her knee. Adelaide imagined from the look on Zuster Wilsma's face that the struggle had been going for some time. She walked over, transferred the tyrant to her own lap, and whispered: 'Go and have your coffee, you must need it.' Then she turned her attention to the child wriggling on her knee. 'Sit still, you bad boy,' she said in a no-nonsense voice. She held him firmly and went on in her careful Dutch. 'The doctor's going to look at my teeth, then I shall have a sweet.' She produced one from her pocket. She had his attention now.

'Then the doctor will look at your teeth, and you can have a sweet too.' She produced another one, and laid it beside the first. 'You hold them.'

He took the sweets, clutching them in his hand, and sat quietly while the professor, with an expressionless face, looked at her teeth. This done, he turned to the child, who looked doubtful.

'You shall have both sweets,' said Adelaide quickly.

When he had gone, the professor looked at her quizzically.

'How do you do it, Sister Peters? Or is it a closely guarded secret? Whatever it is, you lost none of it on holiday, though I can't say the same for your Dutch. There wasn't a single verb in that sentence.'

'I never know where to put them,' she replied airily, 'so I save them up until the end.'

This remark was greeted with roars of laughter from the two men.

'We shouldn't tease you, Sister Peters, your Dutch is really quite good, isn't it, Professor?'

The man at the desk nodded.

'It's so good you shall try your skill on the next patient, Sister. It's that child Lotte Smid. Last time she came she bit Piet!'

The day wore on rapidly; the clinic worked late, and Adelaide stayed to help clear up after the doctors had gone. She listened to the nurses' chatter as she checked dressing packs, and scissors and scalpels, and refurbished the trolleys. It seemed as though she had never been away; her holiday was just a lovely dream. Excepting for the hours spent working together, she saw nothing of the professor during the following weeks. She had quietly refused an invitation to go to his aunt's home with him, and was unreasonably upset when he didn't persist with the invitation.

She persevered with her Dutch lessons, and even the exacting Mijnheer de Wit was pleased with her. It seemed a waste of time to work so hard at something she wouldn't need much longer, but it filled her free time, when she wasn't exploring Amsterdam, or window shopping with the other Sisters. The weather was getting cool, and the wind was chilly. The shops were showing tweeds and pretty clothes for the evening.

One evening at the beginning of October she was going slowly down the Kalverstraat on the way to her lesson. She had plenty of time and was looking rather aimlessly in the shop window. It had been a horrid day in the clinic; Piet had been in a bad temper, and the professor hadn't been there all day. Adelaide stopped at Krause and Vogelzang's to admire a blue velvet dress; very simple, and very expensive. The professor's voice spoke over her shoulder.

'Very charming, Adelaide. Will you buy it tomorrow?'

Her pulses racing, she looked round at him. 'You made me jump, sir.' Her voice was nicely under control, and formal. Whenever he called her Adelaide, she took refuge in formality. But now he smiled at her in such a friendly fashion that she forgot to be stiff.

'Do you see the price?' she asked.

He glanced at the ticket. 'It seems reasonable enough,' he remarked.

'Reasonable!' She made a sound regrettably like a snort. 'Why, for that money, I could send the boys...' she stopped. 'I could go home for another holiday,' she added lamely, and looked anxiously at him. He looked reassuringly vague. For one dreadful moment she had supposed he had heard her thoughtless remark. She sighed, unconsciously—and very audibly—with relief. If he had been as poor as she was, she might have confided in him weeks ago, but to tell a man of his wealth and position would have been tantamount to begging... She went scarlet, just thinking about it.

'I'm on my way to my Dutch lesson; I mustn't be late.' She turned away from the tempting window, and he fell into step beside her.

'Do you mind if I walk with you as far as the Spui?' He took her arm. 'I'm going that way myself.'

'If you're going somewhere, you'll be late,' she said idiotically, very conscious of his arm.

'I?' he queried. 'No, I've plenty of time.'

They reached Mijnheer de Wit's door, and he rang the bell. She wondered where he was going. The faintly mocking look he gave her stopped her just in time from asking. The door gave a faint click, and he pushed it open for her to go in.

'Do you walk back to the hospital alone, Adelaide?'

She paused in the doorway, carefully avoiding his eye. The temptation to say 'yes' was very great, but good sense and the resolution she tried so hard to keep stifled it.

'Jan Hein is calling for me—you remember I met him at Baroness Van Essen's party.' She smiled convincingly, and started to mount the stairs.

Appalled at the ease with which she had lied, she
reflected sadly that he was the last man on earth
she would wish to deceive.

It was pure coincidence that Adelaide should meet
Jan Hein while she was out shopping in the
Leidsestraat the following morning. Rather to her
surprise, he remembered her, seemed delighted to
see her again and carried her off for a cup of coffee
at a nearby café, which was not, she thought, the
kind of place the professor would have chosen. It
was a mean thought, she decided, and tried to make
up for it by being extra nice to Jan. She succeeded
so well that he asked her rather diffidently if she
would go out with him.

'There must be something you want to see. I've
a car. What about a trip to Volendam, or Alkmaar—better still, let's go to the Open Air Museum
at Arnhem. It'll be cold, but I'm sure you'll like
it.'

With almost no hesitation at all, she agreed. She
had a free day in two days' time—a Friday. They
arranged to meet outside the hospital at half past
ten, and parted on excellent terms with each other.

Friday morning was exactly right. The chill of a
Dutch autumn was softened by the still warm sunshine. Adelaide wore her tweed suit and carried a
head-scarf; it might turn cold during the afternoon,

she had learned not to trust the wind since she had lived in Holland.

They took the road to Naarden and stopped for coffee at Jan Tabac, where they sat at one of the big windows overlooking the motorway, and watched the cars stream past. Adelaide, listening to Jan talking about himself, wished it was the professor sitting beside her—not, she thought, that he ever talked about himself. Not to her, at any rate. She gave herself a mental shake and resolved not to think about the professor for the rest of that day. She succeeded in this rather well, so that by the time they had arrived at Arnhem, she was beginning to enjoy herself.

'We'll lunch first, shall we?'

Jan was easing his little Fiat 850 coupé through the centre of the city, looking for an empty parking meter. With unexpected good luck he found one without much trouble, parked, and took Adelaide's arm to steer through a couple of narrow streets into the Nieuwe Plein and the doors of the Riche National. They talked happily through a luncheon they ate with healthy appetites, and Adelaide was surprised to see that it was almost two o'clock when they once more reached the car. She supposed the museum wasn't very large, for the journey back to Amsterdam would take them at least an hour and a half. In this she was mistaken, as she realised when they arrived at the park in which the museum was set up. There were few people about, and they strolled around while she looked her fill at the perfectly arranged farms and cottages, representing every province and age in Holland. By the time she had explored the Zaanse village it was growing chilly, with the sun slipping quickly out of sight behind the evening clouds. She tied her scarf over her bright hair and turned a smiling face to Jan.

'What a lovely day. I have enjoyed it. I might have gone back to England and never seen all this.'

'When do you go?'

They were walking back over the little wooden swing bridge.

'In about a month. The date hasn't been fixed yet.'

'A month's a long time, we must do this again. I've enjoyed it too.' He took her arm. 'Let's get some tea, there's a café at the end of this path.'

It was almost closing time, but a cheerful waiter took their order, and then stood leaning against the door, a model of patience. They were his only customers. The steady flow of foreign visitors had dwindled to a thin trickle by autumn, and no Dutchman was likely to be there at that time of the day—he'd be at home with his life and family, looking forward to the evening meal. The waiter shivered; he would like to be home himself. He watched with well-concealed relief as his custom-

ers got up to go, accepted his tip with dignity, and
sped them on their way.

It was the rush hour in Arnhem. Jan joined the
stream of traffic going out of town, and Adelaide
was glad of their slow progress. Their road ran
alongside the woods and the view was magnificent,
but she knew better than to distract Jan's attention
from the road. He was an impatient driver, and she
found herself comparing his testy manner with the
professor's placid acceptance of the traffic jams
they had encountered when he had taken her to
England. He had remained quite unruffled, merely
making up time between the delays with some fast
driving which had opened her eyes. The traffic
thinned out after a time, nevertheless dusk was
thickening as they turned off the motorway on to
the Amersfoort road. They hadn't gone very far
along it when the car gave a lurch. Jan wrenched
at the wheel and swung back on to the right side
of the road, thankful that there was no other traffic,
and came to a halt.

'That's a tyre gone,' he said gloomily.

Adelaide already had her hand on the door. 'I'll
help you change it.'

He looked at her gratefully, thankful for her matter-of-fact acceptance of the situation.

'Would you hold the torch?'

He busied himself setting up the red triangle behind the car, and had just got the jack in position

when the headlights of an oncoming car, driven fast, picked them out against the emptiness of the surrounding countryside. The lights dipped, and the car stopped without sound within a few yards of them. Adelaide watched the professor, moving much faster than he usually did, get out and cross the road. He came closer to her—so close that she could feel the rough tweed of his jacket against her shoulder. From the gloom above her head he spoke.

'Good evening, Adelaide. Can I help in any way?' He didn't sound very interested.

'We have a puncture, and Jan has to change the wheel.'

He grunted something she couldn't quite hear, and moved away to see what Jan was doing. The two men murmured together, and Adelaide, shining the torch steadily on them, suppressed a shiver. It was getting very chilly, and she wished she had a thicker coat, or even a scarf for her neck. The professor went back to his car and returned with a lantern, directing its beam on to the tyre, then he took the torch from Adelaide's cold hand, and switched it off.

'Go and sit in the car. You'll find a rug in the back. We shan't be long.' He didn't wait to see what she did, but turned away to help Jan.

Adelaide climbed gratefully into the Rolls. It was warm inside, and smelled faintly of good tobacco and well-kept leather. She sat wrapped in the rug, watching the two men working in the pale light of the lamp. She could hear Jan's quick light voice, and the professor's slower, deep one, with an occasional rumble of laughter. She relaxed against the comfortable seat, and allowed herself the luxury of imagining that she was with the professor, and not Jan. She was so absorbed in this delightful but improbable situation that she was quite startled when the car door was opened. The professor looked down at her.

'Jan's ready to go.' He helped her out and took the rug from her and she stood beside the car, feeling awkward, not sure what to say, and bitterly regretting the lie she had told him the other evening. He must think that she and Jan were, at the least, very good friends. She had a wild desire to tell him that this was only the second time that she had seen Jan since Baroness Van Essen's party. She opened her mouth, she wanted him to know about it quite badly. She sneezed.

'You should have worn a warmer coat.' The professor was faintly admonishing. 'I should join Jan if I were you. He'll give you a drink at Amersfoort; you don't want to catch a cold.' He was a stranger, a chance acquaintance giving careless sympathy and advice.

She sneezed again, and said in a small voice:

'It was warm and sunny when we started out this morning.'

'No doubt.' He sounded maddeningly reasonable about it. 'The sensible thing would be for you to go back to hospital and go to bed, but I won't presume to spoil your evening by suggesting it.'

He had walked across the road with her to where Jan was standing, wiping his hands on a piece of rag, and stood looking at them both, smiling a little.

Adelaide, in her turn, smiled brilliantly at Jan, who delighted her by saying promptly:

'Our evening hasn't even started, has it, Adelaide?'

She tightened the scarf around her bright hair and nerved herself to look at the professor. 'Thanks for your help, sir, we shall be able to enjoy every minute of it.'

She whisked into the car, giving a brilliant performance as a young woman about to enjoy a delightful evening with the man of her choice, and waved airily as Jan started the car. The professor looked lonely standing there on the side of the road, cleaning his hands on Jan's rag. Adelaide longed to stop the car and go back to him and fling herself into his arms, and wondered what he would do if she did. Something tactful, she supposed, with a correctness that would be far worse than a downright snub. She stopped thinking and turned to Jan, to ask with her usual candour:

'Do you really want to take me out this evening, Jan?'

'Yes, of course. How about a meal and then a cinema— No, I've a better idea, I'll phone and see if there are any seats for Snip and Snap at the Carré. You'll like that.'

It sounded fun—it would stop her thinking too. They kept up an unflagging conversation until they reached Amsterdam. Jan stopped the car in a busy street near one of the bridges crossing the Amstel. As she got out of the car, Adelaide could see the bright lights of a restaurant on the opposite corner. Jan took her arm and guided her across to it.

'This is the Fredriksplein,' he explained. 'I thought we'd eat here at the Royaal.' It was warm and pleasant inside in the subdued lighting of the table lamps. They sat in the window, watching the fountain in the centre of the square; it looked cold in the light of the street lamps. Adelaide went off to tidy herself and found that Jan had ordered drinks for them both. Hers looked richly red. She sipped it and it tasted as good as it looked. By the time their meal was ready, she was no longer cold, she even felt full of false cheerfulness which carried her successfully through dinner.

The theatre was full, but they had good seats, and Snip and Snap—Amsterdam's favourite comedians—were on top of their form. Adelaide laughed delightedly at their antics, even when she couldn't understand the jokes.

It was late when the show finished, and she refused Jan's offer of a drink.

'I'm on duty tomorrow at eight, there's a clinic—a special one for measles inoculation. We'll be busy. I think I'd better go back now.'

She thanked Jan charmingly for a delightful day, said good night and went into the Nurses' Home, and immediately forgot him. Her last coherent thought before she went to sleep was of Coenraad, standing in the road by himself.

They were all on duty the next morning. By the time the doctors had arrived Adelaide and the nurses had the children in some sort of order. In theory it was a simple enough business. A steady stream of children trickled through the team's well-organised fingers, submitting with stolid charm or howls of rage to the professor's and Piet's swift and expert jabs. Adelaide, busy with the syringes and needles and the repetitive swabbing of countless small arms, stood beside the professor. It was nice to be close to him, even though he didn't appear to notice her: she didn't count the casual 'Good morning' as he had come in. At ten o'clock, she asked quietly:

'Would you like coffee now, sir?'

He plunged his needle into a very small stoical boy, gave him an encouraging smack on his bottom, and threw the syringe into the bin Adelaide had thoughtfully placed to receive it.

'Sister Peters, you read my thoughts!'

She went quickly and called a halt for ten minutes, while a nurse brought in the coffee ready on the small stove. By tacit consent, the nurses moved away with their mugs and biscuits, leaving Adelaide and the two doctors by the desk.

The professor helped himself abundantly to sugar and selected a biscuit with care.

'You enjoyed your evening, Adelaide?' he enquired blandly.

She composed her face into an expression of delighted remembrance.

'Yes, thank you, Professor. We went to the Royaal.'

'The Royaal?' His brow creased in thought. 'Where's that?'

Piet came to her rescue. 'Nice place. Good food, too. What did you do afterwards, Adelaide?'

'We went to the Carre,' she frowned heavily at Coenraad, 'and I liked it very much indeed,' she added in a challenging tone.

He looked taken aback. 'Er—yes, I'm sure you did. I wasn't aware that I had contradicted you in any way. Everyone likes the Carre. I'm glad you enjoyed your evening, I remember you told me how much you were looking forward to it.' He looked faintly mocking. It was a relief to Adelaide when Piet asked her who she had gone out with.

'Jan Hein.'

'Oh, him!' Piet looked at her in astonishment. 'The fellow with the fancy waistcoats? Lord, Adelaide, couldn't you do better than that?'

Adelaide stared at him angrily, regrettably unable to think of anything to reply to this unfortunate comment. That she shared Piet's opinion of Jan didn't help matters at all.

The professor put down his cup. 'Really, Piet, you must allow Adelaide to choose her own friends. Jan's quite a good sort of fellow—only a boy, of course,' he added in a silky voice that set Adelaide's cup rattling in its saucer.

'Are you ready, sir?' She didn't look at either of the men, but turned her back and piled the crockery on to the tray and carried it away. For the rest of the morning she was silent, excepting when it was necessary to talk about the work in the clinic, and when the last small patient had left, and the doctors were ready to go home, it was Zuster Wilsma who took their white coats and answered their goodbyes, Sister Peters having found it imperative to take the drums over to the sterilising room herself. She banged them down on the bench with undue violence and relieved her feelings by slamming the door violently behind her.

The professor was waiting in the passage outside; she was glad to see him wince at the appalling noise she was making, while her heart leapt to see him there. She wondered what he was going to say. But he said nothing at all, merely nodded unsmiling, and went into the sterilising room on some errand of his own.

# CHAPTER NINE

IT was the second week in October, and the hospital ball was to be on the twentieth. There was a good deal of excitement about it, even though work had to go on as usual. It was a Monday morning, cold and blustery and just turned nine o'clock. The professor sat at his desk patiently making illegible notes from the reluctant answers of the young woman he was questioning. She was pale and dirty and uncooperative; he needed a great deal of patience. Adelaide was undressing the young woman's baby; it was pale and dirty like its mother, and very ill. Its puny body was covered in fleabites. It looked unseeingly at Adelaide out of enormous blue eyes, and wailed continuously in a thin parody of a baby's voice. She pinned on a nappy and rolled it in a baby blanket, and said low-voiced to Zuster Eisink who had just come in:

'Get a lumbar puncture trolley ready, will you, Nurse? We're going to need it in a few minutes.'

She unwrapped the baby again as the professor came over and began to examine the scrap with gentle hands. Without looking up he said:

'What do you think, Sister?'

He had a rather nice habit of asking the nurses their opinion before he diagnosed, and as he never laughed at their sometimes foolish answers, but praised them when they were right, they loved him for it.

'Meningitis,' said Adelaide promptly.

'Then I don't suppose I need to ask for the LP trolley,' he said genially, and went to scrub up.

It didn't take very long. They pulled off their masks and gowns, and the professor told Piet Beekman, who had just come in, to take the baby to the small glass-walled cubicle where Zuster Zijlstra could keep her eye on it. Zuster Eisink took the trolley away, and Adelaide found herself alone with the professor, washing their hands at the double sink. She had avoided him as much as possible since her outing with Jan, although, as she told herself frequently, there was no reason for doing so. All the same, she was glad to see Zuster Wilsma come into the clinic. So, it seemed, was the professor.

'The very girl I want,' he said cheerfully. 'Please go to X-ray and ask for the films I need. I've written the numbers down, they're on my desk.' As the door closed he turned back to Adelaide, and asked, 'Did you say something, Sister?'

Adelaide was puzzled; she knew that all the films that were needed had been fetched.

'Yes, sir. I said—but all the films are there.'

'You're quite right, they are. I wanted to talk to you.'

Adelaide struggled to think of something suitable to say to this, failed, and started to wash her hands for the second time, waiting for him to speak.

'Will you come to the hospital ball with me, Addy?' he went on, and added softly, 'And don't cudgel your brain for a mythical escort this time!'

Adelaide started to blush, and would have washed her hands for the third time if the professor hadn't reached over and taken out the plug. She was wildly happy. There was something else too; her hands dripping before her, she turned to face him.

'You knew that Jan didn't come for me…?'

'Yes, I knew.'

She heaved a great sigh of relief and said, without stopping to think, 'I'm so glad; I wanted to tell you it was a lie, but I couldn't think of anything else to say.' She looked up into his face. 'You must know that you're the last person in the world I'd lie to.'

'Yes, I know that too,' he said quietly. 'Will you come?' He thoughtfully handed her a towel to dry her still wet hands, and went on smoothly. 'You leave at the end of the month, I believe? I think it would be a nice gesture if we went together, don't you?'

Adelaide wondered why they should make a nice

gesture, but put the thought aside. She wanted to
go very badly, and she knew she would accept. She
was tired of pretending to herself that her feelings
for him were purely friendly. Once or twice she
had thought that perhaps he was attracted to her,
but common sense told her that he had never really
given her any reason to believe this. He'd kissed
her several times, but that meant nothing when a
man took a girl out. She reminded herself that the
Dutch *Adel* married into their own circle. Doubtless
in his own good time he would marry Margriet. All
the same, he must like her a little to have invited
her. She heard herself accepting in a cool, friendly
voice, and telling him how delighted she would be
to go with him, but in an instant she had forgotten
her role again.

'Oh, I'll buy a new dress!' she breathed recklessly.

She spent several days looking for the dress. She
wanted something really beautiful, and rashly decided to spend some of the money set aside for the
boys' school fees. In the end, she found what she
wanted, a straight, beautifully cut dress in wild silk;
it was in turquoise blue, and cost her far more than
she could afford, but Adelaide didn't care.

The days flew by, and she longed for the night
of the dance, but dreaded each day as it brought
her departure nearer. Her gloom was increased by
the professor's brisk cheerfulness. He seemed to

take it for granted that she was delighted to be going back to England, and even made passing mention of Christmas in her own home. She was too dispirited to point out that hospital ward Sisters seldom got home for Christmas.

On the day before the ball, Adelaide wasn't on duty until eleven. It was a bright, frosty morning, just the day for a brisk walk. She was standing outside the hospital, waiting for a chance to cross the road, when she became aware that Margriet Keizer was standing beside her. Margriet said good morning so charmingly and in such a friendly manner that Adelaide found herself returning her smile. They crossed the road together, and continued along the pavement, chatting about Adelaide's departure in ten days' time. They turned down the Singel, where it was quieter, and walked briskly along in the chilly wind. Adelaide wasn't sure that she wanted to go walking with Margriet, but she saw no way of avoiding it. She had no idea that Margriet had telephoned the hospital earlier that morning and asked when she was to be off duty that day, or that she had spent a long hour waiting in the hope that Adelaide would come out.

Margriet knew exactly what she was going to say; she had been over it a hundred times since that evening, several weeks ago, when she had asked Coenraad to take her to the dance, and he had told her that he intended taking Adelaide. She had seethed with rage, but by a great effort, concealed it, and said nothing more to him about it. But now… She led the conversation round to the dance.

'It's a marvellous affair,' she said gaily. 'Have you a pretty dress for it?'

Adelaide was surprised. 'How did you know I was going?'

Margriet smiled. 'Why, of course I know. I was the one who suggested you went in the first place. Coenraad always takes me, but I told him that this year, just for once, he should take you. After all, you haven't had a great deal of fun while you've been in Holland.' She stole a look at the girl beside her. Adelaide's feeling had been one of disbelief as she listened to her companion, but she had to admit that it was all true. The professor, after all, had barely mentioned the ball to her since his invitation, save to arrange where they were to meet. She felt the blood drain from her face, but managed to smile quite naturally.

'Poor Professor Van Essen, I had no idea…' she stopped.

'Oh, you mustn't say that,' cried Margriet. 'He has a very high regard for you as a nurse. Neither of us mind in the least, we only want you to have an enjoyable evening.'

Adelaide felt numb, but she supposed that presently she would be able to think what to do; at the moment she must concentrate on walking and talking as naturally as possible. Margriet was the last person who must know how much she had been hurt.

'How kind of you both,' she was surprised to find her voice sounded quite normal. 'It was most thoughtful of you to arrange it.' She looked at her watch. 'Now I really must go, I'm on duty in half an hour. I can take this short cut down this alley, can't I?' She was still smiling. 'I expect I shall see you before I go.' She shook hands with Margriet, unaware of the scornful amusement of the other girl at the ease with which Adelaide had been taken in.

'Just in case you don't, Sister, have a good trip home.' She smiled confidingly at Adelaide. 'I'm longing to tell you a secret—I know I shouldn't, but you'll not say a word, I know. I'm hoping to marry Professor Van Essen quite soon.' She watched Adelaide's face become even whiter than it was already. 'I thought you'd be delighted.' Her blue eyes gleamed with triumph.

Adelaide wondered if she was going to faint, she certainly felt most peculiar; she supposed dully that it was shock. She said quietly, 'I hope you will be very happy, *Juffrouw*. I…I must go, or I shall be late.'

She turned into the alley and walked very fast back to the hospital. She had no idea how she got there, or how she changed her clothes, but punctually at eleven o'clock she walked into the professor's office. Piet gave her a startled look and asked her if she was feeling all right; to her relief, the professor said nothing at all. Only later, as they were leaving to go to lunch, he asked if there was anything the matter. His voice was so kind that she had a tremendous urge to burst into tears, cast herself upon his shoulder, and tell him the whole miserable story—which, her matter-of-fact mind told her, was just about the silliest thing that she could do. Instead she said in an unnaturally bright little voice:

'It's nothing, thank you, sir, only that I have a touch of the toothache.'

Adelaide didn't go to her dinner, but spent the hour in her room. She had to think of something, quickly. She caught sight of herself in the mirror; she looked terrible. She remembered that she had told the professor that she had a toothache. Her teeth had never given her any trouble in her life before, but surely a wisdom tooth could flare up at a moment's notice? She started to weave a pattern of lies, for she could think of no other way out of an impossible situation. She went back on duty, and took care to tell the professor that her toothache was no better.

After the clinic was over for the day, and she was alone on duty, she went along to her little office and carefully composed a little note, regretting her inability to go to the dance with him. It would be natural enough for her to do that if her toothache was bad enough, and there would be plenty of time for him to arrange to take Margriet. This melancholy thought caused her to burst into tears and ruin the note, which she had to re-write, then she put it carefully in her pocket and went to supper. She sat near Home Sister, who commented upon her wan looks, so that she was able to tell her, and everyone else sitting nearby, about the wisdom tooth. Home Sister told her kindly to go to bed with plenty of aspirin and she would send a hot drink up presently.

Adelaide prepared for bed, feeling wretched. She had been brought up to have a healthy horror of lying, and now here she was, having told one, forced to tell more every time she opened her mouth. That she wasn't lying for her own benefit hadn't occurred to her. She lay awake most of the night, deciding what she must do, and in the morning, thanks to her sleeplessness, looked worse than ever. She wished the doctors a subdued good morning when they arrived, and in answer to Piet's sympathetic enquiry as to which tooth it was, said:

'It's a wisdom tooth, I think—the left side. I had no idea they could be so painful,' she added for good measure.

The professor regarded her thoughtfully. 'Why not have it looked at? There may be something that can be done to ease the pain.'

Adelaide busied herself with some charts, her head turned away from him. 'No, thank you, sir,' she said carefully. 'I will probably be much better by this evening.'

The morning seemed very long. She avoided the professor as much as possible, and remembered to wince convincingly when she drank her coffee, and put a hand up to her jaw. The professor noticed her action.

'The right wisdom tooth, I think you said, Sister?'

Adelaide stared back at him. He was looking at her very intently. Which side had she told Piet? He wasn't in the room; she didn't know if that was fortunate or not, she was past caring. She no longer had the least idea which wisdom tooth ached. She said recklessly;

'Yes, the right side, sir.'

At dinner time she sought out Home Sister and reported sick.

'If I could just have the rest of the day in bed, Zuster Groeneveld, I'm sure I'll be all right for duty tomorrow. I'm sorry to miss the ball, but I shouldn't enjoy myself, should I?'

Home Sister agreed, commiserated with her on missing all the fun, gave her a fresh supply of aspirins and a cup of tea, and promised that Adelaide's note should be delivered to the professor at once.

The morning had seemed long; the afternoon and evening stretched everlastingly before her. Most of the Sisters were going to the ball. Adelaide sat in bed, admiring them as they came in turn to show their dresses and sympathise with her. When the last one had gone, she got out of bed and went over to her window and opened it wider, so that she could hear the band playing. She stood there a long time, getting very cold, and not noticing it. She got into bed at last, and lay thinking of what she had to do the next morning. When she had planned everything to her entire satisfaction, she burst into tears and after a little, cried herself to sleep.

At nine o'clock the next morning, Adelaide presented herself at Matron's office. The Directrice was busy at her desk as she went in, but looked up and smiled when she saw who it was. She liked Adelaide, who had proved herself a hardworking, sensible, and popular nurse, and had adapted herself to the hospital routine without tedious comparisons between it and her own training school.

She said graciously, 'Good morning, Sister Peters. I'm sorry to hear that you had to miss the ball. It was a great success. I hope your tooth is better?'

Adelaide was momentarily taken aback. She had forgotten about her toothache in the anxiety of getting her speech, rehearsed during the bitter wakeful hours of the night, clear both as to grammar and meaning. She faltered a little, and said uncertainly: 'My tooth? Thank you, Directrice, but I have no toothache.' She ignored the Matron's look of surprise and plunged into the matter in hand, speaking in her heavily accented but fluent Dutch. 'I should like to leave, Directrice. At once. It is a purely personal matter, nothing at all to do with my work, but it is essential that I go home at once. Will you please allow me to go?' She spoke with a quiet desperation that convinced her hearer of her sincerity.

The Matron looked down at her blotter and asked gently:

'Could you explain a little more fully, Sister? You have been happy here, haven't you?'

Adelaide smiled. It lighted up her tired face.

'I've been very happy,' her smile faded, 'and I'm sorry I have to leave like this, although it is only a short time before I am due to go; and I'm afraid I can't tell you any more than I have done, Directrice.'

'Very well, Sister. I think I know you well enough to understand that you are not making this request lightly. But it would be too late for you to go today, in any case.'

'May I go tomorrow? I can arrange my journey today, and pack this evening.' Adelaide hesitated; she still had one more favour to ask. 'Could I go without anyone knowing about it? I know it sounds extraordinary, Directrice, but I have a good reason for asking.'

The Matron frowned. 'I suppose so, Sister—I shall, of course, have to warn Professor Van Essen.'

Adelaide felt her heart hammer at the name. 'No, please…I mean, may I tell him myself? It isn't inconvenient for me to go… Staff Nurse Wilsma is there, so it won't make any difference.'

If the matron heard the desperate urgency in her voice, she gave no sign, but tidied the already tidy papers on the desk before her, and thought. 'So that's it!' She had known the professor for a great many years; she was very fond of him, now she fought a desire to pick up the phone and tell him to come and cope with a situation she couldn't understand.

Adelaide felt nearer to tears. She took a step nearer the desk and said in a beseeching, carefully controlled little voice:

'Please don't tell Professor Van Essen, Directrice.'

'I promise you I will say nothing, Sister. I am sorry that you are unable to let me help you. I should have liked to have done so. But you know best, my dear.' She smiled with real kindliness. 'Do you want to go on duty? Yes?' She nodded dismissal.

Adelaide went to the door, but turned back when she got to it.

'Thank you for being so kind, Directrice.' She couldn't think of anything else to say.

She went to the Sisters' Home from the office, got her cases and put them in her room, then went to the little telephone box in the hall and rang up a travel agency and booked her ticket for the next day without difficulty. It wasn't a time of year when people travelled for pleasure. It was half past nine when she got to the clinic, which was in confusion. One of the children had been sick on the floor, and a boy in one of the cubicles was in the throes of an epileptic fit. The professor was dealing with it as she went in, but he looked up as she crossed the room.

'Ah, Sister Peters, you seem to have arrived at the right moment. Take over here, will you, while I write him up for something, then if you will give it, we can ward him. We'd better have him on observation.'

Adelaide gave some hasty instructions to the nurse to get the place tidied up, and did as she was asked. It was fortunate, she thought, that they were too busy to have time to talk. Indeed there was no time for conversation for the rest of the morning, nor did they take their usual coffee break. By one o'clock the morning clinic was over, an hour late, and they had to be ready in an hour's time for the afternoon session. Adelaide sent the nurses to dinner and whirled around the clinic, changing couch covers, spanking pillows into shape, putting out paper towels, doing all the small jobs vital to a smooth-running clinic. Piet Beekman had dashed home; the professor sat at his desk, scribbling notes in the morning's case papers. He was a methodical man; the morning's work was never allowed to overlap into the afternoon. Adelaide, checking X-rays with less than her usual brisk efficiency, was very conscious of him. She looked up and caught his eye upon her. She would have to say something about the ball; she sorted half a dozen films into the wrong order, and said in an uncertain voice:

'I'm sorry I couldn't go with you last night, sir. I was very disappointed.'

'So was I,' he answered flatly.

Rather discouraged, she persevered. 'I expect you found someone else to go with?' Despite all her efforts, she was annoyed to hear her voice quiver.

'If you mean did I have a sufficient number of dancing partners, Sister Peters—yes, I did.'

She hadn't meant that at all. She longed to ask him if he had taken Margriet, but didn't dare to do so, and—she glanced swiftly at his downbent head. He was sufficiently out of humour to remind her that it was no business of hers, as indeed, she had to allow, it wasn't.

'Your toothache is better, I hope, Sister? Er—
both sides, was it not?'

She dropped the X-rays she was holding, and got
down on her knees, scarlet-cheeked, to pick them
up. When the professor came quietly from behind
his desk and got down on his knees beside her, she
dropped them again. He collected them neatly,
merely remarking:

'The pain seems to have left you in a highly
nervous state, Sister Peters. I think it advisable for
you to see a dentist before you suffer a further at-
tack.'

Adelaide jumped to her feet as he uncoiled himself from the floor. She wished he wasn't standing
quite so close, he seemed enormous, but when she
looked at him his face was as placid as usual. For
a brief, terrifying moment she had thought that he
might have guessed about the toothache.

'Thank you, sir, but I'll go when I get back to
England. My own dentist—it doesn't hurt any
more—remarkable how the pain went...' She realised she was babbling, and stood, for once idle,
watching him piling the X-rays neatly into their
right order. He put them down on his desk and
reached for the telephone. She watched while he
dialled a number, but when he said casually: 'This
man's a personal friend of mine. You'll like him.
I can't allow you to go back to England with even
a suspicion of toothache,' she panicked.

'Please don't.' She could hear her voice high and strained. 'I beg you, please don't. I won't go...'

He put the phone back in its cradle, and said in the silky voice she knew so well; 'Just as you wish, Adelaide.' He got up. 'I'm going to have a sandwich. We'll start promptly, please.'

She watched him stalk out of the room, and listened to him going down the corridor. He was whistling, one of the tunes they had whistled together when they had gone to England. She had been very happy then. She stared unseeingly at the notes in her hand, and gave a great sniff. She would have liked to cry, but there wasn't time, nor was it a suitable place in which to give way to her feelings. She finished what she was doing, then went into her office and closed the door. She still had to write a letter to the professor, explaining why she was leaving. She made one or two vain attempts, but it was useless. She would have to do it in the morning. So she busied herself with the off-duty for the next week, and saw to the stores and stationery and linen lists; it was the least she could do. Just before two, she went back to the office in time to help the two doctors on with their white coats, and told Zuster Steensma to bring in the first patient. The afternoon clinic had started.

When she was at last off duty she went to her room, packed her cases and sat down to write some letters. She wondered what her friends would say when they heard that she had gone without a word of farewell; she would write and explain when she was back in England. After supper she went for a walk with Zuster Zijlstra and bade a silent goodbye to the streets as they passed through them. On their way back they walked down the Herengracht, past the professor's red brick mansion. Several of the windows were lighted; she wondered in which room he was sitting, and if Margriet was with him.

She slept badly, and was glad when it was morning and she could go on duty. She went straight to her office; she had to write a letter to Coenraad, and there would be no time once they started work. After half a dozen attempts she achieved a stiff little letter, and was addressing the envelope when there was a knock on the door and the professor looked in. Adelaide jumped up, feeling guilty, wished him rather a breathless good morning, and managed an embarrassed little laugh when he remarked:

'You don't have to look so guilty, Sister; I'm early.'

He showed no disposition to go, so she stuffed the letter and envelope into her pocket and accompanied him down the corridor to his own office, talking to him in a polite voice, as though he were a stranger she had just met for the first time.

The clinic was slack, so Adelaide was able to do what the Matron had suggested and go to first din-

ner, leaving Zuster Wilsma to finish the clinic with
the two doctors. She sat at the table, eating nothing,
then went to Matron's office and bade her goodbye.
By two o'clock she was at the hospital entrance
with her luggage. Here she gave her letter to the
porter, with instructions to deliver it to the professor at five o'clock, and not a minute before. To
make sure that there was no mistake, she wrote the
instructions on the envelope as well, and watched
the man put it in the doctors' letter rack by the
door, before getting into her taxi. The porter loaded
her cases beside the driver, surprised that she was
leaving. He shook hands with her and offered to
tell the driver where to go.

Adelaide looked at her watch. She had plenty of
time, indeed she was far too early, because, she
admitted ruefully, she had been afraid of meeting
Coenraad again. She made a sudden decision to say
goodbye to Baroness Van Essen; she liked the old
lady, and would be able to wish her a personal
goodbye and give some explanation for her abrupt
departure, for which she would stick to her tale of
urgent private affairs. She gave the address to the
porter, and sat back resolutely looking away from
the hospital where she had been so happy.

She rang the bell hesitantly; it was an awkward
time to call. The Baroness might not be at home.
The door was, however, opened immediately by
Bundle, who ushered her inside the house, and in

answer to her enquiry as to whether she might see his mistress for a few minutes, asked her to be seated while he went to discover if the Baroness was receiving visitors. She was. Adelaide found herself in the same small parlour as before, where Coenraad's aunt sat comfortably before an open fire. She smiled at Adelaide as she walked across the room.

'How nice to see you, Adelaide. Forgive me if I don't get up. What a long time it is since you were here last. Sit down, my dear. I hope you can spare half an hour for a gossip.'

Adelaide chose a chair facing the door, away from the light.

'Please forgive me for calling like this, but I'm on my way to the station, and I found that I had just enough time to come and wish you goodbye.' She paused, aware of Baroness Van Essen's surprised look, and chose her next words carefully. 'I have to go home unexpectedly…'

'My dear child, no one is ill, I hope?'

'No, *Mevrouw*, just a private matter.'

'Coenraad will be disappointed.'

Adelaide wriggled uneasily in her chair, and said at last:

'I haven't told him yet—at least I thought it best to leave a letter.' She struggled to make her voice matter-of-fact. 'He might not understand…' she began, then stopped, for someone was pealing the front door bell. The door banged shut, footsteps sounded in the hall. Adelaide recognised them; she had been listening to their coming and going in the clinic for the past year. She felt as though she was about to faint, but fainting wouldn't help her now. She half rose from her chair, and looked imploringly at her hostess. The old lady smiled at her.

'I do believe it's Coenraad. Now isn't that nice?'

# CHAPTER TEN

THE door opened quickly and violently, and the professor walked in. He shut the door with extreme quietness and stood leaning against it, looking at Adelaide. She had never seen him so angry; his mouth was a thin straight line and there was a vein throbbing at his temple. She deduced, quite rightly, that he was in a towering rage, and waited for the storm to break.

He transferred his gaze to his aunt, and said, in a deceptively mild voice: 'Good afternoon, Tante Anneke—and to you, Miss Peters.'

She caught her breath as he turned narrowed eyes, glinting with rage, on to her once more.

'How fortunate that I find you here. Perhaps you will be good enough to explain this note.'

He waved her letter at her, and she noticed that he was without his overcoat. She looked at the antique wall clock as it chimed the half hour—half past two. She frowned. Why had he got her letter already, when she had been so careful to tell the porter to deliver it at five o'clock? She said in a bewildered voice:

'I thought you had a clinic...'

He stared at her, and she stared back, hiding her agitation as best she might.

'So I have, Miss Peters, none knows that better than you. It just so happened that on this very afternoon I chose to accompany Dr Van Hoven to the front door and collected my post at the same time.'

Adelaide made a small, helpless gesture. 'There's nothing to explain, sir—it's all in my note.'

She picked up her handbag and got up from her chair to take her leave from the Baroness, ignoring him. 'I really must go, *Mevrouw*, or I shall miss my train, and I mustn't keep the taxi waiting any longer.'

The professor didn't move from the door, but said very quietly:

'There is no hurry, Miss Peters. I saw your taxi as I came in, and told Bundle to bring your luggage in and pay off the driver.'

Adelaide found herself shaking with rage at the arrogance of this remark. She stamped her foot into the deep pile of the carpet.

'How dare you?' she asked in a choking voice.

The professor appeared unaffected by this display of temper. Indeed, he looked to her to have recovered his usual good humour. He folded his arms across his chest, and returned her look with one of amused tolerance, which had the effect of inflaming her feelings still further. At this point, the Baroness, until now a silent but interested spectator, got to her feet with a polite murmur and walked over to the door, which her nephew, after dropping a kiss on her cheek, carefully shut behind her. Too late, Adelaide took a few steps across the room, with the vague idea of going through the door too, but the professor put his shoulder against it.

'No,' he said.

She looked at the window, and heard him laugh.

'You'll have to stay and face the music. Won't you sit down?' he continued politely. He left the door and started to walk towards her, and she backed, then blushed furiously as he asked:

'Where are you going? I only want to ask you some questions.'

She knew he was laughing, but carefully avoided his eye and sat down on the extreme edge of a stiff little chair, clasping her shaking hands together.

'Now, Miss Peters, pray help me to understand your note. Are your parents or brothers ill, that you have to return to England so suddenly?'

She hesitated, searching for the right answer, and was almost unnerved when he said, 'The truth, Addy,' in a very gentle voice.

She swallowed the lump in her throat. 'They're all quite well, thank you.'

When he said, 'Do they know you are going home?' she could only shake her head.

'So the "urgent personal matter" concerns yourself?'

She nodded, not trusting herself to speak, her eyes fixed on his waistcoat, while he read the letter through again at his leisure.

'You've written "May I congratulate you and wish you and Freule Keizer every happiness in the future." I wonder why?'

Adelaide swallowed a sob rather noisily and said forlornly: 'You're going to be married.' She looked quickly up at his face, to see him frowning fiercely.

'I can't think how you got to hear of it,' he said carefully.

'Freule Keizer told me the day before the ball,' she gulped. 'She met me as I was going for a walk.'

She was smoothing the fingers of her gloves and heard the professor draw a sharp breath.

'Oh, yes, and what exactly did she tell you?'

Adelaide was past caring what happened next, and repeated Margriet's conversation with her, while he listened in silence.

'She asked me not to tell anyone, but that doesn't mean you, does it?' She spoke to her gloves, not daring to look at him.

He made no reply to this, but said in an understanding way:

'So that explains the toothache.' She nodded. 'So that Margriet and I could go to the ball together,' he continued. She nodded again, and stole a look at him. He was polishing his glasses but looked up and caught her gaze. His eyes were the blue-grey of a Dutch winter sky; she found that she was unable to look away from them.

He said reflectively: 'I do not know why it is so, Adelaide, but you are obsessed with the absurd notion that I should marry Margriet. Oh, I know that it has been common gossip that we should do so, but I have never bothered myself with gossip, nor have I encouraged it. I must make it plain to you that I do not wish to marry her, nor have I ever given her an indication that I intended to do so. It was unfortunate that she told you that she hoped to marry me—it was, how do you say? wishful thinking on her part.' He gave his glasses a final polish and adjusted them carefully. 'What a pity that we should have this—misunderstanding—just as you are on the point of leaving us.'

Adelaide sat silent; there was really nothing to say. She had managed to drag her eyes away from his face, and was once more staring at her gloves. She thought fully how silly she had been; he didn't mind her going in the least. His next words confirmed this.

'I wonder if you would consider coming back for another day or two—until Friday? The clinic is very busy, and you couldn't be replaced until next week. Let me see, it's Tuesday, I shall be taking a day off tomorrow...'

She realised he was expecting an answer. If she had wanted proof that he regarded her only as a useful member of his staff, she now had it. He had come after her because he needed her back in the clinic; that had been the reason for his anger too. She would have liked to have left the house and never see him again, but she had nowhere to go. She forced herself to look at him and answer quietly:

'Provided the Directrice has no objection, I'll stay until Friday, sir.'

'That's a great relief.' He suddenly became very brisk, and went over to the fireplace and pulled the old-fashioned bell rope hanging there. When Bundle answered it, he asked him to get a taxi and put Adelaide's luggage in it.

'I shan't expect you at the clinic this afternoon, Miss Peters; you'll wish to unpack a few things, I expect. May I suggest that you go back now and do so?'

Adelaide got meekly to her feet, and then on her way to the door, said: 'But I must say goodbye to Baroness Van Essen.'

'I'll make your excuses; she'll understand.' He looked at his watch pointedly. 'I really must get back to work.'

She coloured painfully, and went quickly into the hall, where he followed her.

'I'll ring Matron and explain: I'm sure there will

be no difficulty.' He ushered her out to the waiting taxi with all possible speed, and Adelaide found herself driving back to the hospital before having the time to voice her protest at not seeing the Baroness. The professor had seemed to be in a great hurry—for him, of course, it had been nothing but a great waste of time.

Adelaide looked miserably out of the window, and tried not to think.

Adelaide was surprised at the Matron's smooth handling of her return to hospital. She went straight to that lady's office upon her return, feeling rather foolish and quite unable to think of anything to say. The Directrice, however, did not seem to expect any explanations, but made some vague remarks about Adelaide's change of plans, told her that her uniform was ready for her in her old room, and hoped she would go on duty at the usual time on the following morning. Adelaide could only suppose that the professor had given her some plausible reason for his clinic Sister's strange behaviour.

The next day seemed endless. The nurses who had heard that she was leaving on Friday greeted her with dismayed surprise; Dr Beekman who was taking the clinic said very little, however, but gave her his usual 'good morning' and talked trivialities. Once or twice she caught him looking at her rather searchingly. She supposed the professor had told him too, and was grateful to him for not enlarging upon the whole sorry business.

The clinics were not as busy as usual, but Casualty was full, with a steady trickle of burns and scalds, cut heads, and small broken arms and legs. The staff were kept busy, and Adelaide went off duty late and rather tired. After supper Zuster Boot asked her to go to the cinema, and she agreed readily, thinking that it would pass the evening hours. She sat through the programme, watching the film with eyes that saw none of it.

She slept very little that night; she longed yet dreaded to see the professor in the morning. She wished with all her heart that she had never agreed to work until Friday. She dropped into a heavy doze just before she was called, and as she wearily pinned up her hair, looked at the hollow-eyed, tired face in the mirror and had to admit that no man, least of all the professor, was going to give her a second glance that morning.

She greeted him in subdued tones, and felt her spirits sink to an even lower level when Coenraad, asked by Piet Beekman if he didn't think that she looked rather off colour, didn't even bother to lift his eyes from his work, merely saying 'probably' in a voice intended to convey his complete lack of interest. Presently, however, he laid aside his charts and asked her cheerfully if she had been able to change her boat reservation for the next day, and expressed the hope that she would have a pleasant crossing. Adelaide, who had now reached the stage when she didn't care if she had to travel by canoe, replied mendaciously that she was looking forward to it immensely. The professor then suggested, with the air of a man who had taken care of the civilities, that they might as well start work, and was soon engrossed in examining a screaming child with a very nasty impetigo. This seemed a suitable time for Adelaide to slip away to her office; Zuster Wilsma was back from her coffee break and could perfectly well take the clinic for an hour or two. Adelaide had known that it would be difficult seeing Coenraad again, but his bland indifference was something from which she had to escape. Halfway to the door, however, she was halted.

'I should like you to stay, Sister.' He spoke in a voice he seldom used; she knew better than to ignore it, and went meekly back to the desk. He had his back to her, looking at a film on the wall screen.

'Have you checked the Out-Patients' list?' His tone implied that she had not. 'There are several difficult children this morning, so we might as well make use of your powers over the juvenile mind while you are still with us.'

He looked over his shoulder at her, but she did not meet his gaze, but looked at the film with an expressionless face, and said in a very professional voice: 'Very well, sir, just as you say.'

It was a tiring morning. The professor was right, as he so often was. One noisy toddler succeeded another till Adelaide's patience was exhausted. Somehow she got through the morning, and during her dinner hour thankfully wrapped herself in her cloak and walked in the hospital grounds. The air was cold and fresh; she went back to the clinic and made herself a cup of coffee and sat and sipped it until the nurses came back from their dinner.

The afternoon clinic was, if anything, worse than the morning. At four o'clock the professor remarked that if he didn't have a cup of tea and five minutes' quiet, he would be a nervous wreck. Adelaide silently agreed, and sent the nurse for the tea tray, then told her to go and have her own. She put the tray on the desk and turned away to go to her own office, but the professor forestalled her.

'Won't you have a cup with us, Sister? Then we can get on again without delay.' She had no choice but to pour out his tea and put it on the desk beside him. He thanked her without looking up from his work, and she was glad when Piet called to her to bring her cup over to the window with his. She had barely sat down to drink it when the phone rang. The professor answered it and said, 'For you, Sister.'

Adelaide put down her cup and went over to the

desk and took the phone from him; her hand
brushed his as she did so, and the touch set her
pulse hurrying, so that her voice shook as she said:

'Sister Peters speaking.' She was surprised to
hear the Directrice's voice.

'Sister? I see that you are on duty until noon
tomorrow. Professor Van Essen tells me that there
will be no clinic in the morning, and I see no need
for you to come on duty. I expect you will be glad
of a few extra hours before your train leaves.
Perhaps you will come and see me in my office
between nine and half past tomorrow.'

Adelaide said, 'Yes, Directrice,' and 'Thank
you,' and replaced the receiver. The professor had
stopped writing and was watching her. She met his
bland gaze with a look of enquiry.

'You didn't tell me that there was to be no clinic
tomorrow morning, sir.'

'There seemed little point, Sister,' his voice was
cool, 'since you will not be here.'

She looked away, and murmured 'Of course, sir'
then went back to her cooling tea and Piet, who
looked at her unhappy face and plunged into an
account of little Piet's efforts to walk. She didn't
hear a word of it, but his kindly voice soothed her,
so that presently she collected up the tea cups on
to the tray and went to call the next patient with
her usual quiet composure.

The clinic wound to a close about half past five and the professor got up from his desk as the last small patient was ushered out.

'I am going to the wards,' he said abruptly. He nodded at Piet, who was already taking off his white coat, looked austerely at Adelaide and stalked away. The nurses had already started to clear; she plunged into the untidy mass of papers on his desk, intent on getting cleared up and away before he should return. Piet put on his coat and came and stood beside her.

'We shall miss you, Adelaide.' He produced a small parcel from a pocket and pressed it into her hand. 'This is from Leen and me—just to remember us by.'

She took the little packet and thanked him warmly—she was going to miss Leen and Piet and the baby and Mijnheer de Wit and all the friends she had made in the hospital very much. She held out her hand. 'Goodbye, Piet. I've loved working here.' She added wistfully, 'I hope you or Leen will write to me sometimes and tell me all the news.' She hesitated, then went on: 'Piet, I shall be gone before Professor Van Essen comes back—would you say goodbye to him for me?' She saw the surprised doubt on Piet's face, and hurried on: 'I'll write when I get to England.'

'If that's what you want, Addy,' said Piet slowly. Adelaide watched his burly form go through the door, and began with feverish haste to clear up. Coenraad never hurried his evening rounds, so she should have plenty of time to get away. She took a final look round the now spick-and-span office and went to find Zuster Wilsma. To her surprise, all the clinic nurses were waiting for her. They gave her a parting gift and wished her goodbye with a friendliness which warmed her heart.

Adelaide went to her room on the pretext of finishing her packing, but there was little to do, and she sat idle, trying not to think about never seeing Coenraad again, and when at last she went to bed, she cried herself to sleep.

Her haggard appearance at breakfast was put down to her reluctance to leave the hospital. She was generally liked, and her friends' goodbyes were sincere. Back in her room, she put on the green coat and hat, did her face with more care than usual, then went downstairs to the office. It was already after nine—when she had said goodbye to the Directrice, she would go for a walk around the canals.

The Directrice smiled at her kindly and pushing the pile of papers before her aside, talked agreeably for several minutes before shaking hands and saying goodbye. Adelaide opened the door and went outside into the corridor. Coenraad was standing there. He had apparently just come in, for he was wearing a car coat and was even then pulling off his gloves. She hadn't expected to see him again and she stood irresolute in the open doorway, doing nothing. He took a leisurely stride towards her and stretched an arm to close the door, before taking her arm in a gentle, inescapable hold, and started walking down the corridor towards the hospital entrance. Adelaide, unable to do anything else, went with him. Half-formed sentences came and went in her head, but none of them made sense. They went through the door and straight to his car.

'We're going somewhere quiet,' was all he said, and he dumped her unceremoniously in the seat beside his. Adelaide sat very still. The situation had got quite out of hand; they had reached the Munt Toren before she said faintly: 'I'm going for a walk…'

Coenraad eased the car out of a tangle of traffic. 'No, you're not,' he said placidly.

She tried again. 'I should like to get out…' she began.

'And so you shall,' he agreed. 'We're almost there.'

It was no use; she remained silent until presently he turned into the Spui and stopped. He got out and walked around to her side, opened the door and stood wordlessly while she got out too. His gloved hand took a firm grip of her arm, and he piloted her through the archway leading to the picturesque square where the centuries-old Scottish Church stood, surrounded by its close circle of beautiful friendly little houses. It was very quiet; there was no one about. Adelaide stood still and attempted to pull free of Coenraad's grip, but he merely tightened it and started to walk away from the church, around the square, taking her with him. He spoke in his mildest voice.

'We can talk here without interruption. I have something to say to you, Adelaide.'

He glanced down at her. She was looking straight ahead, her hair flamed above her white face, she looked pinched and cold.

'You didn't say goodbye,' he observed pleasantly.

Adelaide looked at her shoes as though she had never seen them before. She felt quite unable to deal with the situation, but did her best.

'I'll write to you when I get to England,' she mumbled.

'What will you write about?' He sounded interested. She gave him a startled look, then stared straight ahead again. What would she write about? What was there to say? That she had been foolish and proud and loved him desperately? She gulped. Two tears started to roll down her cheeks, and she put out her tongue and tried ineffectively to catch them. Then she stopped, because the professor, who could read her thoughts like an open book, had stopped. He turned her round to face him and mopped up her tears with his handkerchief, then put his arms around her and pulled her close; they felt very comforting. She saw his smile and the gleam in his eyes as he bent his head and kissed her. He did it slowly and thoroughly and with evident enjoyment. After a while he said:

'Darling Addy, I love you. I loved you the first time we met. I would have told you a dozen times if it hadn't been for your confounded scruples about my money and title. For a year you've driven me to distraction with your cool friendliness and efficiency and starched aprons.' He kissed her again, quite roughly. 'Will you marry me, Addy?'

She had become quite beautiful; her eyes shone, her cheeks were pink. She smiled adorably at him, and reached up and put her arms shyly about his neck. 'Yes...oh, yes, Coenraad!'

They stood together, very close and listened to the chimes telling the hour.

'I love this little church,' said Adelaide.

'Would you like to be married here, Addy?'

The pink in her cheeks deepened.

'Oh, yes, I would! But can we?'

Coenraad kissed her again. 'Of course,' he smiled. 'I'd like to marry you here and now, but I'm afraid our laws don't allow that.' He looked down at her, his eyes twinkling, and pulled her closer.

'But shall we agree to marry just as soon as all the formalities are dealt with, darling?'

Adelaide nodded happily; he tucked her arm under his, and they started walking slowly back towards the archway.

'Where are we going?' asked Adelaide, not really caring.

They stopped, and Coenraad drew her within the circle of his arms again.

The sounds of the bustling city around them barely penetrated the peace of the little place.

'Why, to start this business of getting married,' he said.

'Does it take long? I mean...can we do it all before I catch my train?'

He held her a little way away from him, so that he could see her face.

'Will it matter very much if you don't catch your train?' he asked. 'It's quite a lengthy proceeding. Will you mind staying with Tante Anneke for a few days, do you think—and then I'll take you home.'

Adelaide looked at him with shining eyes.

'I don't mind where I go or what I do as long as I'm with you.'

Coenraad smiled at her very tenderly, then kissed her softly on one pink cheek.

'Darling Addy,' he said, and took her hand as they went back through the archway together.

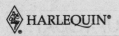

# ANGELS OF THE BIG SKY
## by *Roz Denny Fox*

### (#1368)

Widow Marlee Stein returns to Montana with her
young daughter, ready to help out with Cloud Chasers,
the flying service owned by her brother. When Marlee
takes over piloting duties, she finds herself in conflict
with a client, ranger Wylie Ames. Too bad Marlee's
attracted to a man she doesn't even want to like!

**On sale September 2006!**

# THE CLOUD CHASERS—
Life is looking up.

Watch for the second story in Roz Denny Fox's two-
book series THE CLOUD CHASERS, available in
December 2006.

*Available wherever books are sold, including most
bookstores, supermarkets, discount stores and drugstores.*

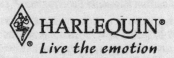

# HARLEQUIN®
*Live the emotion*

If you enjoyed what you just read,
then we've got an offer you can't resist!

# Take 2 bestselling love stories FREE!

# Plus get a FREE surprise gift!

**Clip this page and mail it to Harlequin Reader Service®**

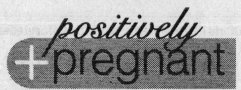

## Silhouette® Desire®

**Introducing an exciting appearance
by legendary
*New York Times* bestselling author**

# DIANA PALMER
## HEARTBREAKER

He's the ultimate bachelor…
but he may have just met
the one woman to change his ways!

Join the drama in the story of a confirmed
bachelor, an amnesiac beauty and their
unexpected passionate romance.

---

"Diana Palmer is a mesmerizing storyteller
who captures the essence of what
a romance should be."—*Affaire de Coeur*

---

**Heartbreaker** *is available from Silhouette Desire
in September 2006.*